HG·11

APR - 4

THE
STAMPEDE KID

Also by Norman A. Fox in Large Print:

Broken Wagon
Cactus Cavalier
Dead End Trail
Ghostly Hoofbeats
Long Lightning
Night Passage
Reckoning at Rimbow
Roughshod
Shadow on the Range
Silent in the Saddle
Stormy in the West
Stranger from Arizona
Tall Man Riding
The Thirsty Land
The Valiant Ones

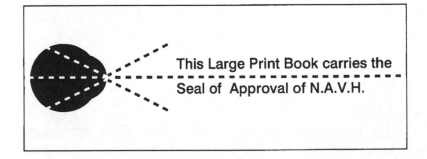

This Large Print Book carries the Seal of Approval of N.A.V.H.

Norman A. Fox

THE STAMPEDE KID

Thorndike Press • Waterville, Maine

Published in 2004 by arrangement with Richard Fox.

Thorndike Press® Large Print Western.

The tree indicium is a trademark of Thorndike Press.

The text of this Large Print edition is unabridged.
Other aspects of the book may vary from the original edition.

Set in 16 pt. Plantin by Warren S. Doersam.

Printed in the United States on permanent paper.

Library of Congress Cataloging-in-Publication Data

Fox, Norman A., 1911–1960.
    The stampede kid / Norman A. Fox.
      p. cm.
    ISBN 0-7862-6152-8 (lg. print : hc : alk. paper)
    1. Railroads — Design and construction — Fiction.
2. Clergy — Crimes against — Fiction. 3. Brothers —
Death — Fiction. 4. Revenge — Fiction. 5. Large type
books. I. Title.
PS3511.O968S73 2004
    813′.54—dc22   2003066771

To
ARCHIE JOSCELYN
for many reasons — but mostly
because he is my friend. . . .

As the Founder/CEO of NAVH, the only national health agency solely devoted to those who, although not totally blind, have an eye disease which could lead to serious visual impairment, I am pleased to recognize Thorndike Press* as one of the leading publishers in the large print field.

Founded in 1954 in San Francisco to prepare large print textbooks for partially seeing children, NAVH became the pioneer and standard setting agency in the preparation of large type.

Today, those publishers who meet our standards carry the prestigious "Seal of Approval" indicating high quality large print. We are delighted that Thorndike Press is one of the publishers whose titles meet these standards. We are also pleased to recognize the significant contribution Thorndike Press is making in this important and growing field.

Lorraine H. Marchi, L.H.D.
Founder/CEO
NAVH

* Thorndike Press encompasses the following imprints: Thorndike, Wheeler, Walker and Large Print Press.

1.

The prairie was a dreary waste today, an endless sea of sage shuddering under the sweep of the wind — a wind that had been sired in Canada to moan across the naked rangeland miles with the teeth of winter in it. The icy blast sighed dismally along the narrow street of Caprock, battering against the bleak false fronts of that huddle of buildings breaking the prairie's vast expanse, stirring dust devils into turbulent life, screaming a strident song beneath the eaves. Yet the tall man who shouldered into the wind as he marched along the boardwalk was oblivious to the sting of it.

He was a man whose thoughts had turned inward, excluding all else, and there was purpose, grim purpose, in his footsteps as he strode through the gathering gloom toward the meeting hall on the cowtown's ragged outskirts. Craggy and leather-faced, he had the look of one who'd bedded with a blizzard and known nature intimately, her smiling face and her scowling face. About him today there was a solemn gravity, the only outward indication that he was all too aware that he might be on his way to pronounce his own doom.

His name was Henry Harlow McGrath, but Montana knew him from the Marias to the Yellowstone as Hellvation Hank McGrath, a circuit-riding sky pilot who might christen a baby and thrash a bully all in the same morning, doing each chore with a zealot's thoroughness and impartiality. A two-fisted fighting preacher, this Hellvation Hank. Now there was a new battle for him; but it was not just another fight. This time it was a matter of choosing between loyalty to a friend on the one hand; his duty, as he saw it, on the other.

That was just what it amounted to. But his decision was made, and Hellvation Hank shouldered purposefully into the meeting hall. This was his church in Caprock, when he chose to use it as such; an ungainly building of clapboard and tarpaper, yet as sturdy and serviceable as Hellvation Hank himself.

The interior of the place was narrow and dark. Benches served as pews, while a raised platform with a table was the only altar. The room was packed with people, and there was a restless stir as he made his entrance, as though all the excitement that

8

gripped Caprock these days were concentrated here.

Excitement! Glimpsing his friend Tyler Whitman in the congregation, McGrath reflected that here was the shadow of things to come. Wherever Whitman was, there'd be excitement. Tyler Whitman was president of Montana-Pacific, the roaring railroad that had pushed across the untamed Dakotas and into Montana until now the end of steel was already nearing Caprock. That was why Tyler Whitman was here. There'd be a new boom in Caprock with grading contracts for those who wanted them, and beef contracts being let to supply the hungry railroad crews with food. Today the town was a magnet to draw the reputable and the disreputable, the forces of good and the powers of evil.

All these things the sky pilot knew. And they were in his mind as he took his stand behind the table, a bony man who looked older than his forty-odd years. Funereal black garbed him, a concession to his calling. From habit he dragged a Bible from a cavernous pocket of his shapeless coat, but he did not open it. Instead he stood with the Book in his hand, his face calm and expressionless.

"I'll use no text tonight," he announced, and the packed people turned silent before his voice. "It's not the Sabbath, and it's not a sermon I'm here to preach. I bring you a warning."

He knew how to chain their attention, did Hellvation Hank. He could twist the devil's tail when occasion demanded, and he'd shoveled out his share of brimstone from a score of crude pulpits. But it was no nebulous evil from another world that he'd planned to speak about when he'd called this meeting in Caprock. A gusty something that might have been a sigh rippled across his congregation, and he waited until it had its way.

"You are a happy people," he said then. "You know that a dream long cherished by most of us is to be realized. The railroad is coming to Caprock. And though there is some good in all that is evil, and some evil in all that is good, still I have weighed this significant news and found it to be good news. We will see a boom here while the end of steel is at Caprock, and we'll see a more enduring prosperity afterwards. Think what the railroad can mean!

"Ranchers will be able to ship cattle to eastern markets without losing the profit on the way. Mines will open in the Big

Thunders, and those mountains will surrender their riches. A new day will dawn, a day we have long awaited — a day I have prayed to see, since it will mean the coming of law and order to this land. For you who are gathered here, there will be material rewards. For me there will be the satisfaction of seeing this country become settled and orderly. Our Eden is almost within reach. But like the Eden of old, it has its serpent. Our serpent is a three-headed one."

He paused, studying the sea of faces before him, hearing the uneasy creak of benches, seeing neighbor stare covertly at neighbor. He raised his voice to the pitch he used when he promised eternal damnation for the wicked, eternal happiness for the chosen.

"Three men," he said bluntly, "will stoop to any means to keep Montana-Pacific from crossing the Big Thunders. They are selfish, these three; men who care nothing for the greater good, but think only of themselves. Their names are known to me. Part of their plans are known to me. How did I discover these things? you wonder. I have befriended many men in my time, for, by the grace of God, I am sometimes His instrument of mercy. One such man, a

11

fallen brother whose name I cannot mention, first told me of these three. The secret is mine."

He paused again, and there was a subtle change in his voice, while a zealot's fire gave life to his bony face.

"I do not say these three are here," he went. "It makes no difference, for my word will reach them. I give them one week to mend their sinful ways! Let them come to me within that time and prove their repentance and the matter shall be forever forgotten. If they decide, instead, to go on as before — I shall have no choice. In that case, one week from tonight I shall stand here and name them to you, expose them for what they are. Good night, my friends. May God go with you."

He was down from the platform before a man moved and, as was his custom, he stationed himself at the door to shake each person's hand as the congregation filed out.

Suddenly the people were pouring from the meeting hall, an excited, babbling throng, and Hellvation Hank smiled to himself, knowing he'd stirred them as he'd never stirred them before. The first out was gray-headed Thackery Weaver, editor of the Caprock *Tribune*, the cowtown's weekly newspaper. Weaver was scribbling notes as he hurried along, so intent upon his task that he did not see McGrath's outstretched hand.

After the editor came Tyler Whitman, the railroad builder, a soldierly man who looked uncomfortable in white silk and broadcloth, wearing it with none of the grace of sun-tanned, poker-faced Kurt Ormond, his chief construction engineer, who was with him. Both men had come to Caprock only two weeks before, outriders for the iron horse they represented. Whitman took McGrath's hand.

"Sorry I've been so busy since I landed in this town that I haven't had time for a man-sized talk with you, Hank," Whitman said. "It was a treat listening to you tonight. The years have changed you, friend. Who'd guess that twenty some years ago we were both eating the dust of the drag down on the Brazos — a couple of uncurried cowhands? And who'd think that I'd turn out to be a railroad builder, and you a gospel shouter?"

"It's been a long time, Ty," said Hellvation Hank, and the warmth of genuine affection was in his smile.

"That kid brother of yours," Whitman said. "He must be quite a size now. What do you hear from Matt?"

Something crossed Hellvation Hank's face, something that was no more than a shadow yet left the sky pilot older with its passing. "Matt never was much of a hand for writing," he said briefly.

Broad-shouldered Curly Bottsinger, owner of the stage and freight line that threaded all that wild country from the Dakota border to the Big Thunders, brushed past without a word. After him came fancy-dressed Hoyt Durham, proprietor of the Golden Slipper Saloon. McGrath regarded the man with open surprise as Durham paused to light a cigar.

"Didn't expect to find you at church, Durham," he said cordially.

Durham shrugged, and there was something of a sneer in the gesture. "Why not?" he countered. "I might as well lock up my place and throw the key away any time you start twisting the devil's tail. You sell a convincing bill of goods, preacher. Never could figure out why a man would rather listen to you when any one of my percentage girls could —"

It wasn't so much what Durham was saying but the way he was saying it that darkened McGrath's face with anger. "Stop!" he shouted. "You can't mention

14

wickedness in the very shadow of the House of God!"

"To hell I can't!" Durham retorted, and spat toward the open doorway.

McGrath hit him then, his fist lashing out to crash against Durham's chin, a solid blow. The freshly-lighted cigar showered sparks as it arced away, while Durham sprawled backwards upon the ground. The saloon-owner came to his feet with murder in his eyes, and a derringer was in his hand. But McGrath was upon him before he could use it, wresting the tiny gun away and hurling it into the gathering shadows. The fight went out of Hoyt Durham very suddenly then. He contented himself with a barbed glance at the sky pilot.

"You'll pay for that some day, gospel-grinder!" he snapped, and stalked off.

Tyler Whitman, who'd taken half a step forward at the beginning of the short-lived fracas, frowned as he watched Durham depart, while Kurt Ormond stood as inscrutable as ever. But now another man was barging from the doorway, a semi-bald old cattleman who plucked at McGrath's sleeve with one hand while he crossed palms with Tyler Whitman at the same time.

"What the dickens is all the mystery

about, Hank?" the cowman demanded. "What's this palaver about three sidewinders? You meanin' me, you riddle-tongued hymn singer? You know dang well I'm ag'in' the cast-iron cayuse that Ty, here, figgers he's gonna run across this range!"

"You're just as narrow between the horns as you always were, Storm," Whitman observed, grinning.

"Ain't no secret about how I stand!" the cowman snorted. "You think I want my Deadman range cluttered up with hoemen? And that's what the railroad will bring. You mark my word! Most o' these cattlemen can't see no further than a beef contract for feedin' gradin' crews. They'll savvy how much good the railroad is doin' when they find squatters on their waterholes!"

McGrath listened to Storm Herndon of the H-in-a-Hat spread with a good-natured smile, proof enough that he considered the rancher's outburst no true indication of the man's real attitude, any more than Tyler Whitman had.

"You're a long way off your range, *amigo*," the preacher observed. "Now that Whitman's here, a lot of ranchers are in Caprock to angle for a railroad beef contract. That wouldn't have fetched you, would it, Storm? And how's that girl of yours?"

"Tara? Kickin' over the traces again. Says she's fed up with eastern schoolin'. Writes me that she's comin' home next spring whether I like it or not. Stubborn, that gal is!"

"Wouldn't take after her dad, would she?" Whitman murmured, still grinning, but Storm Herndon was bustling off, merging with the crowd. Singly and in groups the rest of the congregation paraded down Caprock's street until only Hank McGrath and the two railroad men stood in the dusk. Tyler Whitman quietly clipped a cigar.

"Those three you mentioned, Hank," he said. "I'd be mighty interested in their names. Since the government's promised to subsidize the first railroad to cross the Big Thunders, it's turned into a race between us and Central Western. With that outfit bucking us every step of the way, it's trouble enough putting the rails through. I've got ways of catching my own rats, Hank, but I'd like to know who you were driving at."

Hellvation Hank's leathery face clouded. "Do you suppose I haven't thought of that,

17

Ty?" he asked. "We're old friends, and those three are striking at the very heart of the thing you're trying to do — the thing I want to see you succeed in doing. Not for your sake or mine, but for Montana's. Even when I was walking down here late this afternoon, I was making a choice, deciding where my duty lay. But I've got my work, too, friend. I've got to save men from the wickedness within them. Even those three. They'll have their chance to redeem themselves."

Whitman nodded. "Maybe so," he conceded drily. "I figured that would be your stand, knowing you as I do. But I've got a trouble-shooter, name of Dan Callishaw, down the line who knows the right way of saving gents from their own wickedness. But I don't suppose we could ever see eye to eye on *that*. So long, pard."

"If you change your mind about naming those three," Kurt Ormond put in, "you'll find us at the Drovers' Rest, McGrath."

Hellvation Hank favored him with a calculating glance. "I won't be changing my mind, Ormond," he said. "Not for a week, anyway."

They shook hands all around, but Hellvation Hank clung the longest to Whitman's fingers, for they were two old

18

friends who'd shared their formative years together before each had taken a different trail. Then Whitman strode away, and with him went Kurt Ormond; and Hellvation Hank stood alone, watching them go. The sky pilot bent his own footsteps toward the isolated shack which was his home in Caprock.

The place, built of clapboard, stood beyond the town, lonely and forlorn, the wind slipping through it. When McGrath lighted a kerosene lamp on the split-log table in the center of the single room, the flame flickered wildly. The table, a stove, a bunk, and a few chairs furnished the shack. The sky pilot busied himself at the stove, building a fire mechanically, for the magnitude of the challenge he'd made this night filled his thoughts.

Had he said too much about the three, he wondered, and about the original source of his information? If there was fear within him, characteristically it wasn't for himself. But he was remembering the man who'd first warned him of the trio who threatened the Montana-Pacific railroad. Perhaps he shouldn't have mentioned that man, that walker of dark ways. He hadn't wanted to jeopardize the fellow.

It was while he was turning the matter

over in his mind that he heard the faint creeping sound outside. It was no more than the scrape of a boot sole against the hard-packed earth, but it brought McGrath to the door, where he stood framed by the light behind him as he peered into the murk. A man paused not many paces away.

"Who is it?" the preacher called, and then he recognized the silent figure standing just at the edge of the rim of light. Not an hour before he'd asked three men to come to him, and already one of them was there. To repent — or to take revenge? The sky pilot didn't know, but it was like Hellvation Hank to give the man the benefit of the doubt.

"My seed seems to have been cast upon fertile ground," he said joyfully. "I had a hunch that of the three, you would be the one who would come to me first. Won't you come in, my friend?"

His answer came in blossoming gun-flame, and the flat crash of a six-gun blended with the wind and was lost. Lead smashed into the sky pilot's chest. Stunned by the tearing, burning impact of the slug, Hellvation Hank spun, teetering on his toes in the doorway for an endless moment before he fell full length upon the ground.

And as he sprawled there, the assassin who'd come creeping was already slipping away into the darkness.

There was blood on Hellvation Hank's fingers as he clutched his shattered chest, and there was a great sadness in his heart — the sadness of Him who said: "Father, forgive them; for they know not what they do." But the fighting heart of Hellvation Hank had its say too, and its voice was the voice of anger and frustration.

He was dying. He'd tended too many dying men not to know that his own hour had come. He'd defied the evil forces who threatened the coming of steel, and those forces had struck him down. Now he knew he'd made a grave mistake by not giving their names to Tyler Whitman. And now all his thoughts focused on the need to warn his friend somehow, to name the three so that Tyler Whitman might guard against them.

There were writing materials in the shack, but when he tried to crawl toward the doorway, he found his strength was not enough. He thought then to scratch three names in the earth, but the ground was hard-packed and defied his faltering fingers. He tried once again to reach the doorway, but his writhing only succeeded in working the Bible out of his pocket, where it lay in the yellow splash of light, the wind fingering the pages.

And looking upon the Book, the light of inspiration glowed in the dimming eyes of Hellvation Hank. There *was* a way to leave a message after all! Flipping the pages he knew so well, he turned unerringly to certain passages. These he marked in the lamplight, marking them with the only means at hand, smearing the passages with his own life blood. And his task was finished before his fingers stiffened, and his pain-racked body lay still. . . .

That was the way they were to find him when morning came and the first snow lay like a shroud, blanketing Caprock and the range beyond — sifting softly over the body of Hellvation Hank McGrath. . . .

2.

Down where the turgid Rio Grande cut its
tortuous way to the Gulf, they had a lot of
names for men like young Matthew
McGrath; none of them complimentary. Yet
there were many like him in that vast land
of the Lone Star — youngsters with a flair
for danger, a love for the wild life; soldiers
of fortune following their own dark star,
laughing and loving and fighting with the
same whole-hearted recklessness that was
both their weakness and their strength.

But Texas was far behind Matt McGrath
when his greatest adventure had its beginning. The grave of Hellvation Hank was six
months old, and the snow had gone from
it, when he rode up the trail into Montana.
Now April smiled upon Caprock range.
The rolling prairie, freed from its icy fet-
ters, moon-mellowed and alive with the
first faint stirrings of spring, spread before
him as he followed the newly-laid twin
rails toward the distant town where his
brother was buried.

Yet here on this alien range, the stamp of

Texas was still upon Matt McGrath, for his saddle was low-horned and double cinched, and his lass rope was under forty feet in length. A man used to brush country swings a small loop. His chaps, tied behind his saddle now, were designed for a thorny country too. The heaviest bullhide had gone into their making, and the tapaderos were more than ornaments.

The man himself was as serviceable-looking as his gear. Saddle-whacking had hammered his muscles into stringy leanness, and something in his tanned face proved he'd crowded a lot of living into a few brief years. His were rocky features, ageless and inscrutable, and his mouth was that of a man who could be a good friend or a ruthless enemy, whichever circumstances dictated.

Whistling a toneless tune a hundred bedded herds had known, he paralleled the rails which swung in an abrupt curve to cross the trestle spanning Crowfoot Gulch, east of Caprock. That was where things began to happen. He'd come unscathed through the land that had belonged to the Kiowas, the Choctaws, and the Chickasaws, breasted the Red, the Brazos, the Washita, and all those treacherous streams that intersect the north trail from Texas.

Yet danger awaited him at trail's end, Matt McGrath knew, for his was a rendezvous with destiny. There'd been plenty of time for thinking as the weary miles had unreeled behind him, and he'd given due consideration to the perils which would probably attend his mission. But danger would have its beginning at Caprock, he presumed, and the town was still many miles away.

Thus he had no inkling of peril as he forced his mount onto the track at the end of the trestle; no premonition that death might be lurking there. Neither was he annoyed because his mount, a splendid looking bay with plenty of speed and bottom, snorted and pawed, patently skittish of that spidery framework of timber and steel. Biding his time, Matt spoke soothingly to the spooked horse. His patience saved his life.

"Easy, boy," he was murmuring. "Easy the—"

His word broke in the middle. In the center of the trestle a blue flame lashed upward like a devil's forking tongue, and the silence of the night was wrenched asunder by a terrific blast, echoing and re-echoing along the gulch. Dynamite! There could be no mistake about that. A giant's hand might have slapped horse and rider, hurling them backward bodily just as the trestle bulged at its middle, then caved drunkenly to break in the boiling smoke.

But that was only the beginning of havoc. Timbers rained like toothpicks from the sky. On the fringe of that deadly downpour, Matt came out of his saddle, his first astonishment at finding himself still alive changing to a tremendous anger.

This sabotage was aimed at the Montana-Pacific, of course. That fact was self-evident. But it didn't change the fact that the explosion had almost claimed *his* life. No man could blast Matthew McGrath off his horse! Jerking a gun from beneath the slicker he wore, he ran to the lip of the gulch. Smoke and dust stung his eyes as he peered downward, but faint moonlight filtered through the murky veil. And there just below him, on a ledge of sorts, a man hunkered in the shelter of an outcropping of rock, his back to the Texan.

The fellow was perhaps ten feet down. Matt didn't take time to gauge the distance, nor to wonder if others might be nearby to side the man below. The fellow's presence in the gulch was proof enough that he'd had a hand in the dynamiting. Gun in hand, the Texan leaped, landing almost on top of the man. Had he landed squarely, there would have been no fight. As it was, the man he was after instantly jerked around, his eyes wide with alarm. Wrapping brawny arms around the Texan, he threw his weight against Matt. Then the two of them were down, locked in deadly embrace, rolling and struggling on the narrow shelf.

There was no chance for Matt to use his gun, but his adversary couldn't reach a weapon either. As they waged their silent, deadly fight, the Texan caught glimpses of the other's face — a round face, seamed and leathery, with a rim of gray hair showing beneath a sombrero which had been jammed tight in the struggle. This fellow was an oldster, but he was stocky of body and mighty of arm. Matt McGrath, in his mid-twenties, had the advantage of youth, but his adversary was all whang leather, and fighting with a desperation that made them equals in those first few moments.

Yet the Texan would have subdued the other shortly, for there was a lot of steel in the lanky length of Matt McGrath. And the difference in years would have told against the older man once the fellow had expended his first strength. But, wriggling eel-like from Matt's grasp, the oldster lunged to his feet, tripping over his own spurs as he did so. For a moment he tottered on the edge of the ledge, clawing at the air, his face frantic in the moonlight. Matt was to remember the man as he looked then. Then the oldster vanished from view, and Matt pulled himself forward to see the man bounding and rolling downward into the gulch.

The slope was gradual enough. The gray-headed man was going to stop up against a bush below, none the worse for his experience, if luck favored him. There might still be a second round to this fight. Matt, his anger still burning, ached to close with the man again, finish the thing properly. He would have followed him, but at that instant he was jerked erect by a distant, unmistakable sound — the mournful wail of a locomotive!

A train was coming! Which meant the train was racing down the track straight for the dynamited trestle and destruction! Had the engineer heard the sound of the explosion and guessed what lay ahead? Matt didn't know, but the chances were that the train's crew had no inkling of the peril ahead. It had been many minutes since the explosion, and the train might have been several miles away when the dynamite had let go.

Frantically Matt clawed up the slope, starting a miniature avalanche of rocks and dirt behind him until he finally stood panting and disheveled on the rim of the gulch. Forgotten was the man below who would be scurrying away unchallenged. Matt was running, sprinting desperately down the track, spurred by the need to signal that train, stop it before it reached the gulch where death waited.

His horse had bolted. He found the bay a quarter-mile from the trestle, stomping nervously near the low embankment of the grade. Matt vaulted into the saddle at once, using spurs and the quirt that had been dangling from the saddle-horn to force the mount up the embankment and between the rails. No time now to be patient with the animal. Already those rails were humming, and the locomotive's head-lamp penciled light on a distant bluff. Matt peeled off his slicker. Waving it wildly as he spurred forward, he prayed that the engineer would be wide awake.

Straight toward the Texan a bell-stacked engine roared, a hurtling juggernaut of the night, and it took all his skill as a rider to hold the horse on the track. Straight toward him that locomotive came, bathing him in the light of its head-lamp. Blinded by the glare of it, he had to trust to his other senses now. He heard the squeal of brakes just as he jumped his skittish horse off the track. Then the train — a dozen flatcars of steel with one passenger coach and a pusher engine behind — slid to a noisy, screeching stop.

The conductor was on the ground instantly, and even the engineer deserted his cab. But it was to the tall, soldierly-looking man who was the first to alight from the passenger coach that Matt turned. The look of a leader had marked Tyler Whitman for what he was. He made a commanding figure in the faint moon-light, hatless and silver-haired, stern-jawed and altogether formidable.

"Trestle out — over the gulch ahead!" Matt panted as he came out of his saddle. "Dynamited! Had to stop you —"

Tyler Whitman took the news without any great show of consternation, but the railroad builder's fingers were like steel biting into Matt's arm. "You're sure?" Whitman barked. "Who did it? Did you see them?"

"Couldn't say who did it," Matt con-fessed. "I tangled with one of 'em, but he got away. I was all set to take his trail when I heard your whistle. That bridge is shore enough busted!"

A dozen men had crowded down the coach's steps, and Whitman, all action, spun upon them.

"Trestle's out over Crowfoot Gulch!" he snapped. "You, Hanson! There's an emergency telegraph layout in the tool shack back a piece. Uncouple the pusher engine and back down there. Notify division headquarters about this at once. Tell 'em I want a clean-up crew here by sunup with everything we'll need. Wait! Hammersmith! Arm six men and have a look around the gulch up yonder. If anybody's still hanging around there, I want 'em brought back — alive. While you're there, inventory exactly what we'll need. . . ."

There were other orders, and the lieutenants of the railroad builder dispersed in half a dozen different directions, each with an assignment to complete. He could get action, this Tyler Whitman. There was something of awe and admiration in Matt's eyes as they followed the man. And while he watched, someone touched him, and he turned to confront a girl who had come from the coach.

She was bundled in a greatcoat that did little to hide the alluring femininity of her.

Dark hair flowed about her shoulders, framing a face that was pretty enough to take Matt's breath away. He was a six-footer, this Texan, and she came just up to his chin, he noticed, but she had a certain poise that gave her added stature. Her eyes were blue, he guessed, and big — but not with fear.

"I'm Tara Herndon," she said. "I want to thank you for what you did tonight. You saved the life of every one of us."

He took her hand, finding it small and firm, her grip altogether mannish. "I just happened to be along," he muttered. "It might have been anybody." Patently confused, he groped for firmer ground. "Say, the boss of this railroad outfit is some gent!" he said with unfeigned admiration. "Reminds me of the sod-buster that cut six holes in the wall of his shack. Seems he had six cats, and when he yelled 'Scat!' he wanted something stirrin'."

There were other things he wanted to say, and not about Tyler Whitman, for even at this, their first meeting, he had a curiosity to know all there was to know about Tara Herndon. He would have been content to make their conversation endless, but Whitman, his orders given, unwittingly broke the spell of the moment by appearing suddenly, his hand outstretched.

"And now I've time to thank you properly," the railroad builder said. "For myself — and for the Montana-Pacific. I am Tyler Whitman, head of the road, and I owe you a great deal, sir. If there is any way I can repay you, any service I can render in return —"

Matt pawed for the makings, and a broad grin broke the rocky bleakness of his face. "Wa-al now, I could use a job," he hinted.

Tyler Whitman sized him up, inventorying the lanky leanness of him from his sombrero to his high-heeled boots, and taking special note of the hang of his guns. And because Whitman had once been of this whang-leather breed himself, he smiled.

"What can you do?" he asked.

"On a railroad? Shucks now, I reckon a branding iron would grow rusty, and you can't take the kinks out of a cast-iron cayuse with a pair of spurs. That leaves my fists and my gun to work with."

"A trouble-shooter? I could use a dozen of them, feller. It's a tough job, man. There's Central Western trying to beat us, and other forces buck us as well. Sabotage, such as this sample you seen tonight — agitators in our construction crews keeping our men from doing a day's work — beef for the grading crews never arriving — leeches debauching our work crews in the end o' steel towns. Do you want any part of our kind of work?"

"You've just hired yourself a man, looks like," said Matt.

"Very well," Whitman agreed, and was the man of action at once. "You've got a horse. You can skirt the gulch and get into Caprock while we're still bogged down here. You'll find Dan Callishaw, my trouble-shooter, there. Report to him. Tell him I've hired you as his assistant. He'll find plenty of work for you to do."

One of Whitman's assistants was at his elbow with something to report. But the railroad builder, about to turn away, swung back to face Matt. "Your name?" he asked.

"Name?" said Matt. "A man picks up a heap of names on a heap o' trails. I packed a Bible up from Texas. I used it in a trail town where there was no preacher to say any words over a dead gal. They called me the Gospel Kid from then on, and the name seems to have stuck. But if you've got to have something more official to put down on the records — list me as Matt McGrath."

"McGrath!" Whitman echoed, his eyes

widening. "I savvy! You're Hank's kid brother. Now I know why there was something familiar about the lean look of you!"

The Gospel Kid grinned. "I got the Bible you sent me, Whitman, but it was a long time coming. Me, I never had the same address for much of a spell. Likewise I got the letter. It said Hank had declared a one-man war on three skunks who was buckin' the railroad, and that he was shot down before he had a chance to name 'em."

"I thought you'd want the Bible," Whitman explained. "It was about the only thing Hank owned. He had a Texas address penciled beneath your name on the family record page. I took a chance that anything sent to that address would reach you."

His eyes narrowed with a new thought. "You're here to look for the men who got Hank! You were just joshing about working for me."

Something icy glinted in the Kid's eyes. "I crave to look along my gunsight at three gents," he admitted. "Them three are buckin' the Montana-Pacific — and now I'm working for the railroad. You see how it adds up, Whitman? One job sorta fits in with the other. But there's more to it than that. You said in your letter that Hank craved to see a railroad in this country. It was his dream — but he didn't live long enough to see it come true. I'd sorta like to have a hand in the building of that railroad for Hank."

His voice softened, and the ice went from his eyes. "You knew him, Whitman, but you never knew me," he said. "No two men, born of the same woman, was ever so different as me and Hank. He chose his trail, I chose mine, and those trails was a heap apart. But he was my brother. I'll be seein' you in Caprock, boss."

He would have turned away then, but he felt the tug of Tara Herndon's glance. She was mounting the steps of the coach, but she was glancing toward him, and the look she gave him was stony and carried disgust in it.

Just for an instant their eyes locked and then, with a toss of her head, she was gone inside the coach. The Kid stood staring, frowning in puzzlement. It troubled Matt, that look of hers, for it was entirely opposite to what her attitude had been before he'd identified himself. He wanted mightily to know what had changed her, and he might have hurried after her to find out. But he was working for the railroad

36

now, and he had his orders. Shrugging, he stepped up into his saddle, and the night swallowed him.

3.

Long after the Gospel Kid had vanished into the night, Tara Herndon sat in the lighted coach, peering out into the darkness in the general direction he had taken. Huddled in the seat, her chin lost in the folds of the greatcoat she wore, there was something elfin about her at the moment. But her eyes were afire with anger. The tall Texan who had ridden into her life, and out again, was in her thoughts, and there was a certain irony in the fact that she'd liked him instinctively when she'd first looked upon him. But that was before she'd learned his name and his purpose.

Hellvation Hank McGrath's brother! She'd known the fighting preacher, of course, just as every other soul on the Deadman range, where her father's H-in-a-Hat ranch was situated, had known him.

He was part of most of her memories, was Hellvation Hank, for he'd frequently stopped at the H-in-a-Hat when his circuit brought him to their range. As a small girl she'd perched upon his knee. And in a rough land with no law and very little religion, she had gotten all the Sunday School that she'd ever had from his lips — Biblical stories couched in simple language, truths told so that a child might understand them.

Thus Hellvation Hank had become her first hero. With an instinct entirely feminine, she had quickly sensed the difference that set him apart and loved him for it; loved him as she loved cantankerous old Storm Herndon. It was not only because there was a gentleness to Hank McGrath that had appealed to her, or a depth of understanding to the man that had made him like a second father to her. It went deeper than that, a profound admiration that had been based upon respect.

Yet Tara Herndon's kind of man wasn't necessarily a hymn-singing, soft-spoken creature. Old Storm Herndon had come to that range when his nearest neighbor had been a hundred and sixty miles away. All of Herndon's worldly goods had been piled in a wagon, and his wife had been on the seat beside him.

Together they'd built a sod shanty on the naked Montana prairie, and Tara had been born in that hovel. Sarah Herndon had died there, a scant year later. After that there'd been an old Crow Indian woman who'd been mother and nurse to the girl. And Storm Herndon had sought solace from a grief he never betrayed in a frenzy of work that had finally made the H-in-a-Hat what it was this day.

Not that the going had been easy. There were marauding Sioux at first, and roving Crow with an eye for anybody's horses. Other ranchers had come, and at their heels came those vultures of the range, the rustlers.

There had been nights when Storm Herndon had left his home — a new, bigger home that had replaced the sod shanty — his eyes purposeful, his rifle cocked. There had been dawns when the cottonwoods along nameless creeks had borne strange fruit that swayed in the breeze, men who stared with eyes that no longer saw. And upon such a foundation of toil and danger the H-in-a-Hat had been built.

It took steel to do what Storm Herndon had done across the years, and part of that oldster's iron had been bequeathed to his daughter. She knew the whang-leather breed of her father and respected it. When the man of her choice came along, he would be of that breed. But there would be

40

something of Hellvation Hank in him too.

And there lay the seed of her anger. For Matt McGrath, flesh of Hank's flesh and blood of his blood, was in no other way akin to Hellvation Hank. Tara knew too much about Matt McGrath, things she had heard from Hellvation Hank. If she had needed a confessor in her formative years and found one in Hank McGrath, then the sky pilot, who'd taken the troubles of all humanity to his own bosom, had had dark moments of his own when the urge to confide in someone had unlocked his lips and heart.

Now Hellvation Hank was dead, his great heart stilled until eternity rolled around. A letter from her father last fall had given Tara the news, and her grief had been so great that no tears had come to assuage it. Hellvation Hank was dead, and his brother had come to avenge him. And, remembering things Hank had told her, Tara hated Matt McGrath for his intent.

"Why couldn't he have stayed in Texas?" she wondered fiercely. "Why did he have to fetch his infernal gun to Montana? Can't he see that the very thing he is going to do is the last thing Hank would have wanted?"

It was then she became conscious that Tyler Whitman was there in the coach,

41

standing beside her. "May I?" he asked, and nodded toward the seat opposite hers. When she smiled he took his place across from her.

Seated, he looked less soldierly than before, as though he had kept going until his orders were given, driving himself by a force of will that had led to this inevitable aftermath. There were new lines etched in his lean face, and his smile was wan.

"A long night ahead," he observed. "We're doing everything in our power to rush things along, but the train is stalled here until the trestle is repaired. If it takes too long, I'll arrange to have a stagecoach sent out from Caprock by the old road so that those who wish will be able to go on."

She shuddered. "So long as we are still alive, we've hardly cause for complaint," she said. "Has this sort of thing been happening often?"

"Too often!" he said grimly. "And it's only part of what the Montana-Pacific has had to buck. That's why I've been meaning to talk to you. I noticed you here on the train when I came aboard back at division headquarters, but it wasn't until afterwards that I discovered who you were. You see, you could do a great deal to help the Montana-Pacific."

"I?" she cried in astonishment, her surprise so great that it wrung another smile from Whitman.

"Yes, you. You're Storm Herndon's daughter, aren't you? That means you're probably the only person in the world who has any influence over him."

"You know my father?"

"Know him well," Whitman replied. "Would you believe that once he and I and Hellvation Hank McGrath rode for the same outfit down in Texas? You knew Hank, of course. Your father and I were friends before you were born, shared our blankets and tobacco before Storm Herndon ever set eyes on the girl who became his wife."

"I've seen you before —" she said vaguely, reaching into the mists of memory.

"Each of us took a different trail," Whitman went on. "Storm hankered for a ranch of his own, and he did manage to get a few cows under his H-in-a-Hat iron. He trailed those cows to Montana, and your mother went with him. Hank drifted his own way, too. A queer youngster, Hank was; a man who heard a call. That call took him to Montana. If Storm Herndon wanted to improve the breed of cattle,

Hank wanted to better the breed of people. Great men, both of them.

"Me, I drifted too. The Union Pacific was being pushed through in those days, and I became a meat-fetcher for the road, working under Buffalo Bill Cody. But before the rails reached Promontory Point, I'd gotten into the actual railroading end of it, and found the work I wanted to do for the rest of my life. It wasn't long after that I came to Montana and paid a short visit to Hank and your dad. You were only a tot then, and it's small wonder that you scarcely remember. But when I looked upon this range for the first time, I knew what my great job was going to be. That was fifteen years ago. Today I'm seeing that job accomplished — my railroad crossing Montana!"

The look she gave him bore a new respect. "And a fight every step of the way," she said.

"Aye, a fight every step of the way," he agreed. "And the irony of it is that one of the men I'm fighting is as good a friend as I ever had — your father."

"Dad!"

"He has no love for the railroad," Whitman said. "He feels that the coming of steel means the coming of sodbusters,

44

homesteaders, the end of the open range. Perhaps he's right, but railroad or no, the homesteaders are coming anyway. That's as much a part of destiny as was the fact that the Indian had to give way before the first settlers, and the buffalo had to vanish with the coming of the cow. Storm Herndon can't change that. But in the meantime, the railroad is going to mean prosperity for the cattlemen in many ways. But Storm can't see it that way."

"He can hang on to an opinion," she agreed. "He's stubborn, Dad is." And she wondered why he smiled, for she couldn't know that Storm Herndon had used that same word to describe his daughter. Then a new thought filled her with horror. "That dynamiting tonight! You don't mean — !"

Whitman shook his head. "No," he said. "I'll never believe that Storm Herndon would stoop to that kind of fighting — not against me, anyway. But there's more to building a railroad than throwing a trestle across a gulch, or laying a mile of steel a day. Graders have to be fed, Miss Herndon, and it takes beef — plenty of beef — to feed them. So far we've been getting our beef from the Caprock ranchers, but soon we'll be into the Deadman country. Your father is king there — king by right of his priority as the first settler, and by virtue of the fact that Storm Herndon would be a leader wherever he was."

"I see," she said slowly. "He could buck you by refusing to sell beef to the railroad and by talking the other Deadman ranchers out of the idea."

"And if he does, he'll be betraying his neighbors," Whitman pointed out. "He'll be keeping them from doing a nice piece of business while the Montana-Pacific is under construction. And he'll be keeping the road from going through — which means he'll be hurting his neighbors and himself badly in the long run. Cattle cars don't run the tallow off critters on the way to market like a trail drive does. And cattle cars move a lot faster, too."

She gave him a long, measuring glance. "I'm beginning to understand now," she said. "You want me to talk Dad into playing your game."

"You make it sound sinister," he said with a certain dignity. "That isn't what I meant to ask of you. You see, I was out in Caprock last fall and made arrangements to supply the grading camps. I won't be needing beef from Deadman range for a few weeks more, but Storm agreed — then — to gather a herd between himself and his

46

neighbors and to deliver that herd on a certain date which isn't too far distant now. But since then I've heard that he's become more rabid in his hatred for the railroad. I'm wondering if he'll fulfill his contract. I'm wondering if you'd help me see that he does."

Tara pondered over his words for a full minute, and when she lifted her eyes to the railroad builder's, her gaze was level enough. "Dad hasn't said much about the railroad in his letters," she said. "As far as that goes, his letters are generally scribbled on a sheet torn from his tally book. If the dates weren't changed, they'd be practically the same letter. The weather is stormy, or the weather is good. The calf drop is what it should be, or the calf drop isn't what it should be. No, Dad's no letter writer. But I'll tell you this much, Mr. Whitman. If he made an agreement with you, he'll keep it. And if he's the least bit hesitant, *I'll* see that he keeps it."

"That's all I ask."

She gave him her hand, and the grip of it sealed their compact. "I won't lie to you," she said. "As far as future beef deliveries are concerned, I'll make no promises. I'll have a talk with Dad as soon as I get home, hear his side of this railroad idea. And whatever stand Dad thinks is best, Mr.

47

Whitman — that will be my stand."

"You," he said, "are sure enough Storm Herndon's daughter."

"And you're Storm Herndon's friend. I think we'll get along."

"I'm sure of it," he agreed. "If Hellvation Hank were still alive, he'd talk some sense into that old mossyhorn. But Hank's gone, and both of us have lost the best friend we ever had. What did you think of his kid brother?"

"You knew Matt before?" she asked casually — too casually.

"He'd just been born when Hank and I and your dad rode together. When I saw Hank in Montana, he told me a little about the boy. And I've heard the name of Matt McGrath a few times since. Texas men spin a few yarns about him."

"Then you know what he is!" she cried, aghast. "You know that he's as different from Hank as night is from day! And still, with your railroad up to its ears in trouble, you hire *him!*"

"I'm taking a chance that any kin of Hellvation Hank's would have part of Hank in him," he said simply.

She dropped the subject with a thud that was almost audible, and there was something in her face that deterred Whitman, a

48

wise man in many ways, from mentioning it again. But as Tara stared off into the darkness once more, she was plagued by a disquieting thought.

She had no earthly use for this Matt McGrath, known to some as the Gospel Kid, a sobriquet that fitted him not at all. Why then, Tara wondered savagely, should she even be thinking of him? And why should she be wondering, in spite of herself, when her trail would cross with the Kid's again?

4.

Saddle-weary, the Gospel Kid had slept upon the prairie, and he arrived in Caprock the morning after the explosion at Crowfoot Gulch to find a town such as Hellvation Hank had never known.

Gone was the drowsiness of yesteryear. The railroad had come to Caprock, and the streets were thronged by a thousand men — graders and gamblers and gunmen, steel-layers and mule-skinners, bridge builders and beef barons, and men whose callings were shady and nameless.

Cattle had created an empire there in eastern Montana, and on the crest of that boom, Caprock had been born. Yet in its wildest days this town had known nothing more raucous than the revelry of a ranch crew celebrating payday, the bawling of a corralled beef herd awaiting a buyer's inspection, the crash and thunder of guns as horse-and-rope men settled sundry differences in the dust of the street. But now a medley of alien sounds made for discord.

Spring rains had turned the street into a

muddy mire. Along it moved ponderous freight wagons, the teamsters drawing upon copious vocabularies to heap blistering invective upon the toiling horses. Engines puffed and screamed at the sidings and made the air foul with blanketing smoke. Hammers and saws pounded and rasped as new buildings were reared, while the drumming of boots along the boardwalks was an incessant thing. Caprock had blossomed into a sordid kind of splendor.

Standing in the street, the Kid regarded it all, his sombrero thumbed back to reveal a shock of corn-colored hair, his thumbs hooked in his gunbelt. There was something here that was both attractive and repulsive, and the Kid was fascinated and disgusted at the same time. Yet it wasn't religious leanings that caused his qualms. He carried Hellvation Hank's bloodstained Bible in his shirt-front, but his own trail had been a smoky trail, and his ways were violent ways.

But grim business had brought him to Caprock, and sightseeing had no part in it. Shrugging aside his contradictory reactions to this railroad boom-town, he headed for the new pine-boarded building that was the railroad's office, a beehive of activity. There a squat, red-faced, red-headed Irishman, who sat hunched over a telegraph instrument, gave him the information he wanted.

"Dan Callishaw?" the telegrapher repeated. "Shure and it's up at the Drovers' Rest ye'll be finding him. And if yez'll be so kind, yez can tell him Key O'Dade says there's a telegram here for him."

"I'm his new assistant," the Kid said. "I'll take it to him."

Key O'Dade regarded him from beneath a green eyeshade, and the Kid had the feeling that he stood naked before the Irishman's searching glance. "Then here it is, me bucko," O'Dade agreed, extending a slip of paper. "Seeing as it's from Tyler Whitman, confirming the hiring of ye, I guess you're the man to be delivering it."

The Kid found the Drovers' Rest easily enough — a shabby, two-storied building that had had its day of glory when beef had first been king there. After a word with the desk clerk, he climbed the dusty, carpeted stairway to drum his knuckles upon a door.

"Come in," a voice bade him, and the Kid stepped inside — to find himself confronting a leveled gun.

In that room with its pine bureau, the inevitable pitcher and bowl — both cracked — and the iron bedstead that had seen better days, the man with the gun was the predominating figure — a short, stubby fellow of indefinite age with a bulldog jaw and the flaring nostrils of a fighting man. The sun had turned him to leather, and the wind had carved him along bleak lines, as though he were some piece of animated sculpture, the handiwork of nature in a savage mood.

"Who are you?" he asked testily. "And what the hell do you want?"

"Reckon this wire will explain," said the Kid.

Dan Callishaw laboriously read the slip of paper, managing to keep an alert eye on the Kid the while. Then he pouched his gun, casing the weapon by some legerdemain that won the Kid's quick approval. Grinning wryly, Callishaw extended his hand.

"Plumb sorry," he said. "A man has to be spooky to keep on living in Caprock. But if Ty Whitman hired you and sent you to me, you're on the right side of the fence. McGrath, is it? No kin to Hellvation Hank?"

"*Hermano*," said the Kid. "My brother. You knew him?"

Callishaw shook his head. "Heard a heap

53

about him, though. The steel hadn't pushed as far as Caprock last fall, and I wasn't sent here until after Hank died. Whitman and Kurt Ormond, his chief engineer, were around here at the time, lining things up. Have a drink?"

The Kid might have accepted, for trail dust was thick in his throat. But his eyes were growing more accustomed to the semi-gloom of this musty room, and they widened with astonishment. He'd seen a few odd things in his time, had the Kid; but never anything as out of place as the article standing in the corner nearest to the bed. It was hardly a thing a man would expect to find in a hotel room, for it was a headboard for a grave — a new headboard made of white pine, a precious commodity in that prairie country.

But it was the painted lettering which really amazed the Kid, for it read:

HERE LIES DANIEL CALLISHAW
Born October 2, 1847
Died April 18, 1889
HE WAS WARNED,
BUT HE WOULDN'T LISTEN

Callishaw grinned at the Kid's surprise. "Now," said the trouble-shooter, "do you see why I unleather my gun before I open the door?"

"God!" said the Kid. "What's the idea — ? April eighteenth! Why, that's today!"

"A warning from The Three," Callishaw explained. "It's their way of telling me to git out by today or take the consequences. I found yonder thing here in this room a couple weeks ago."

The Kid was suddenly electrified. *"The Three?"* he repeated.

"It's a name we've got for the bunch that's causing Montana-Pacific all its grief. Ty Whitman started calling them The Three after Hellvation Hank warned this town that three snakes were out to stop the steel."

"And they sent you that?"

"I reckon. Pretty, ain't it? I find it right handy for scratching matches when I hanker to smoke in bed."

But the Kid wasn't fooled by the flippancy in Callishaw's tone. The man was worried — gravely worried — and his fear was the more significant because this Dan Callishaw, the Kid decided, wasn't a man who spooked easily.

The Kid eyed the headboard again, and a quick suspicion narrowed his eyes as a thought struck him.

"How about that first date?" he wanted to know. "How could they know the date of your birth?"

"Reckon anybody hereabouts could send me a birthday present if they had a mind to," Callishaw explained. "Thackery Weaver, the gent who runs the Caprock newspaper, gave me some publicity when I first hit town. He talked things over with me and got the detail. See it."

He'd pinned a newspaper clipping upon the wall, and he indicated it with one stubby finger. The Kid, moving closer, ran his eyes over it. The heading read AMONG US TODAY. Obviously it was a regular feature of Thackery Weaver's newspaper, a column presenting prominent newcomers to the town. It began:

"Dan Callishaw, a representative of the Montana-Pacific Railroad, who has lately been assigned to duty in Caprock, has had a colorful career. Callishaw first saw the light of day in Indiana, where he was born on October 2, 1847. . . ."

There was much more to it, a lurid description of the subsequent doings of Dan Callishaw, trouble-shooter. The Kid skipped through it rapidly, his curiosity on one point satisfied. Anybody in Caprock who'd read that article would have learned the birth date of Dan Callishaw — and hence might have prepared the weird wooden warning.

"You think they'll try for you today?" the Kid asked.

Callishaw shrugged. "Maybe. Probably bluff, though. It's one thing to name the day of a man's death; it's another to make sure he dies on that day — especially if he's been warned and is keeping his eye peeled. But you can be damn sure it gives a man something to think about!"

The Kid had to agree. It was a forceful sort of warning, and its inference was easily understood. But he dismissed the matter from his thoughts, eyeing his superior woodenly. "Where do I start to work?" the Kid asked.

"Work?" Callishaw repeated. "There'll be work for twenty like us, from now on. It's been a bad winter, and M.P. just barely got beyond Caprock. But a new season's opening, and we'll be heading for Lazura, the next town, fast. Then's when hell will start to pop."

"Me, I thought it got a fair start last night," the Kid remarked drily.

"Yeah? Ty mentioned the dynamite job

in his telegram. That was just an eye-opener! We could use a troop of soldiers, but the government can't see our need for them, even though a batch of blue-coats are hunkering on their haunches down at Fort Yellowstone. The Union Pacific had soldier protection. That was because the Indians were lifting hair in them days. We're fightin' an outfit just as crafty and just as tough!"

He paused, arching one eyebrow. "You eat yet?" he asked abruptly. The Kid shook his head. "Go get some grub under your belt, McGrath," Callishaw ordered. "Then we'll catch the work train out to the grading camp. Kurt Ormond's at end o' steel, and he's complaining that the crews are dissatisfied and sullen. We'll see if we can stomp out the snake that's keeping 'em that way."

That suited the Kid, for inactivity weighed heavily upon him. With a brief, "Watch yourself, feller," he left in search of a meal. The M.P. had a commissary in Caprock, but it was on the edge of town, he learned, and there was a restaurant nearer, a gloomy place smelling of dirt and grease.

Inside, the Kid found a secluded table for himself. The restaurant was filled and waitresses were hurrying everywhere. While the Kid waited, he took the Bible from his shirt-front and fished into his pockets for a pencil stub and a scrap of paper. The Bible was at his elbow, but he didn't refer to it as he scribbled three verses absently:

"And there went out a champion out of the camp of the Philistines, named Goliath of Gath, whose height was six cubits and a span."

"When Herod the king had heard these things, he was troubled, and all Jerusalem with him."

"Then one of the twelve called Judas Iscariot went unto the chief priests . . . to betray him."

For a long time the Kid frowned upon the words he had written, and even after food was placed before him, his mind was still upon the riddle of those three references.

In his pocket was the letter Tyler Whitman had written when he'd sent Hellvation Hank's Bible to Matt McGrath. That letter had been damnably uninformative. Hank had threatened to expose three men who were bucking the coming of the railroad. Hank had been murdered before he could name the three. That was the size of it.

Three men — At first Matt McGrath had seen no significance in those three bloodstained passages in his brother's Bible. And then he'd begun to read a meaning in them, for those three passages referred to three Biblical characters. Matt McGrath knew little about the Book. But he'd taken to studying it after that, to the utter amazement of certain operators of dubious dives along the brimstone border. And slowly Matt had begun to understand why those passages had been marked. That was when he'd packed his turkey and taken the long trail north — in search of three men . . .

Goliath was one of them — a man of great strength . . . But Samson had been a strong man, too. Why hadn't Hellvation Hank marked a reference to Samson instead of Goliath, Matt wondered? But as he munched his food in Caprock's restaurant, the Kid thought he saw the answer. Samson had used his strength for a good cause — Goliath had championed evil. There was the difference. And there was a clue for the Gospel Kid.

Herod? The king of Judea had been a

puzzler for the Kid. He'd searched long and diligently for the key to the character of that man, dead almost two thousand years. Herod — crafty and cruel and unscrupulous — an evil king, jealous of his sovereignty — a red-handed man who'd had lesser men do his killing for him . . .

And Judas — the betrayer. There was the simplest of the three to decode.

There was one other significance in those three references, the Kid decided. Obviously the three he sought did not have Biblical given names — a fact which narrowed the search. No Pete or Jake or Joe had struck down Hellvation Hank. If such had been the case, the sky pilot would have marked a reference to Peter, Jacob, or Joseph, and simplified the mystery that was Matt McGrath's sole heritage.

His hunger satisfied by bacon and eggs and coffee, the Kid came to the street again. If there was a man in Caprock who might know what enemies of the Montana-Pacific had traits resembling those of Goliath, Herod, and Judas, that man was Dan Callishaw, whose job was to battle The Three. He'd ask Callishaw about them right away, the Kid promised himself.

A thousand sounds beat against him as he skipped nimbly across the muddy street.

Two freighters, their wagons wheel-locked hub against hub, cursed each other roundly. And on a nearby corner a drunken man, his shirt-tail out and flapping, lifted a gun and fired into the sky, punctuating the shots with a declaration to all within earshot that he was a curly wolf and therefore entitled to howl. And on that street where sin strode boldly, personified by men whose mouths were too grim and women whose cheeks were too red, that roaring gun attracted no attention.

Truly, the Kid observed as he climbed the gloomy stairway to Dan Callishaw's door, this town was feeling its oats. And then, mindful of Callishaw's hair-trigger alertness, he called loudly.

"It's me, McGrath, Dan," he said before he stepped into the room.

Dan Callishaw was there, but now he was a shapeless sprawling thing, heaped in a corner, and there was no life in him, for a bullet had torn off the top of his head. In falling he had somehow crashed against the headboard tilted against the wall, and his body pinned it there, half concealing it.

But the Kid could still remember that last line: HE WAS WARNED, BUT HE WOULDN'T LISTEN.

5.

Many businesses had boomed in Caprock with the coming of steel, but Hoyt Durham's Golden Slipper Saloon had reaped the greatest share of the golden harvest. Always a place where a man might enjoy dubious pleasures, its trade had been many times multiplied by the influx of railroad workers who sought the solace of the bottle, the green baize, or the painted smiles of percentage girls — at a price.

A long bar ran the length of the Golden Slipper, and two sweating barkeeps toiled to attend to the thirst of those who lined it. There was a spacious floor for dancing, while a gambling wing, adjacent to the main room, hummed to the click of the roulette wheels, the clink of fingered chips, the incessant slap of the pasteboards.

Oil paintings adorned the walls of the saloon proper. Most of them depicted seminudes, and one in particular held the place of honor, a huge painting called "The Lady of the Nile" which portrayed a voluptuous, sultry-eyed woman who stretched full length upon a leopard skin, a diaphanous wisp of cloth flowing about her.

There was a second story to the Golden Slipper. And on this upper floor were the rooms of the percentage girls and the entrance to another room as well — a room that no more than a dozen men had even been inside. It was built above the level of the first story and below the level of the second story, and it was Hoyt Durham's private office, a place of luxurious furnishings as befitted the man who ruled the shadowy side of Caprock town and whose ramifications extended to the range beyond, into the very shadow of the Big Thunders.

Three men sat in that room on the morning of Matt McGrath's arrival in Caprock.

One was Hoyt Durham, dark-skinned and dandified, a thin-faced man with a wisp of a moustache and a nervous habit of preening it with one jewel-bedecked hand. Garbed in a gambler's funereal black, his clothes were a concession to his inordinate vanity. His boots were hand-sewn, his knee-iength plantation-style coat was of the best broadcloth, and his flat-crowned black sombrero cost more than a cowpoke made in a month's riding. He was a little man, a good six inches under six feet, but there was something in the restless grace of his whipcord body that suggested the latent strength of a caged cougar and the same ruthless ferocity.

The second man was Curly Bottsinger. The smallness of Durham only accentuated the bulk of Bottsinger, for the broad-shouldered freight-line owner was a huge hulking giant, shaggy and powerful and for all the world like a rampaging grizzly. Broad of face as well as of figure, Bottsinger had the look of a man given to stormy passions, a creature ruled more by impulse than by reason.

A lamp lighted the room, even in the daytime, for, situated as the room was, it had no windows. A window would have betrayed its location from the outside, since any opening into the room would have had to be out of line with the general plan of the building. The third man sat in the shadows, just beyond the fringe of yellow light.

He was studying the two, this third man, and his thought at the moment was that Hoyt Durham was the deadlier of the pair in spite of the primitive savagery of Bottsinger. Yet Bottsinger looked murderous enough just then.

"I had to wait," Bottsinger was explaining to the others. "This gent that come along was in the room with Callishaw for quite a spell. I tried to listen to what they was jawin' about. As much as I could get was that this jigger had been sent to side Callishaw — another trouble-shooter. I didn't want to hang around too close to the door for fear one of 'em might come bustin' out. I hid in the hall until the new jigger left."

"Yes . . . ?" the third man prompted him.

"After that it was plumb easy. I knocked, and Callishaw let me in. He had that old Peacemaker of his in his fist, and he wasn't in no hurry about pouchin' it. Jumpy as a bare-footed Piute in a blizzard, he was. 'I just come in from end o' steel,' I said to him. 'I got news for you, Dan.' He relaxed some then, puttin' his gun away. He turned toward the dresser and I guess he was going to pour hisself a drink. I let him have it and got out in a hurry."

"Positive he was dead?" the third man asked.

"Plumb positive," Bottsinger insisted. "Weren't no doubt about that."

"Anybody notice the shot?"

"Reckon not. The clerk wasn't at the desk. And some drunk was blazin' at the sky down on the corner, and there was a cap or two bein' cracked out in the alley behind. What difference did another shot make?"

The third man settled back in his chair contentedly, his eyes thoughtful, his smile easy as he listened to the sounds that reached him through the thin walls.

"Business is good, eh, Hoyt?" he observed. "Gentlemen, you're a pair of unmitigated scoundrels. Look at you, Hoyt — bucking Montana-Pacific, fighting the road tooth and nail, and all the while you're lining your pockets with railroad payroll money spent over your bar and gaming tables. And you, Curly — you're getting fat on grading contracts and the money you're paid to haul freight past the end of steel. Biting the hand that feeds you."

"So?" Hoyt Durham said, smiling without humor. "Business was good before the railroad came, especially if a man lifted a little beef in the dark of the moon as a sideline. But what happens when the road is finished? The boom is over, and law and order comes to the Caprock country. There'll be no place for my kind then."

"Me, I hate every damn tie they lay," Bottsinger exploded savagely. "Look at the

67

cinch thing I had! If a man wanted something hauled on or off this range, he paid my price — and liked it. And if some jigger got the notion of starting a rival freight line, things happened to that gent. But now trains are running as far as Caprock already. I'll be bankrupt once this road goes through. I wish to hell Tyler Whitman had been dumped into Crowfoot Gulch last night with that load of steel on top of him! It was only fool luck that saved him after me and the boys blasted that trestle!"

"The main thing," said the third man, "is that the trestle was damaged enough to keep a train from crossing it. So long as rails and ties and supplies can't be brought out to end o' steel, M.P. is tied up just as thoroughly as though Ty Whitman did crash into the gulch. That's why he'll be moving heaven and earth to get that trestle repaired in double-quick time. But a few of the boys are going out to Crowfoot tonight to see that the trestle isn't fixed too fast."

"They better do a better job than we did last night," Bottsinger growled.

The third man still smiled — the satisfied smile of a man whose allies are his pawns, to be moved at his discretion and for his eventual good. Bottsinger folded one hairy fist and regarded it truculently. Durham stirred restlessly.

"What's next?" the saloon-owner asked. "Think we ought to send that new trouble-shooter a headboard, giving him about a week to get out of the country?"

"That headboard idea's no good!" Bottsinger scoffed. "It didn't make Callishaw run."

"The headboard idea," the third man explained patiently, "has a psychological value, Curly. You wouldn't understand about that. Its value is twice as great now since Dan Callishaw wouldn't be warned and had to die. Savvy? The next man to get one of those wooden warnings is going to remember what happened to Dan Callishaw. And he's going to know that that warning means exactly what it implies."

"And I'm saying that we should send one to that new trouble-shooter that Curly heard up in Callishaw's room," Durham insisted. "We want to get rid of him pronto."

"Not yet," the third man decided. "Not unless the opportunity is laid right in our laps and is too good to pass up. The fellow will probably walk softly once he learns what happened to Callishaw, anyway. Our job right now is at end o' steel. Curly, you'd better get out there again. The boys can handle that business at Crowfoot Gulch tonight without you. It looks like winter is really over, and Whitman's order will be to drive — and drive hard. You keep the men stirred up enough so they'll do about half their work. Tell 'em M.P. is going broke, and they'll never be paid. Tell 'em Central Western is paying better money. Tell 'em anything you please. Every delay means Montana-Pacific is that much nearer to being licked."

"And C.W. is that much nearer to crossing the Big Thunders first," Durham added. "That will please *you*, eh? And us, too. Montana's big enough to have a railroad without the steel running through the Caprock country to spoil our business. Got anything lined up for me?"

"Later," the third man promised. "There's a chore that will be cropping up after a while for those hell-for-leather boys you keep out in the hills. I'll let you know when the time comes to put them into saddles."

Curly Bottsinger came to his feet and moved in his ponderous fashion to the wall that separated this office from the barroom below. A leather flap, no more than four inches square, hung on the wall about three feet above the floor. Crouching, Bottsinger lifted the flap to peer through two eyeholes bored in the wall.

In this manner he was looking down into the barroom through the eyes of "The Lady of the Nile." The picture was a trick affair and an ingenious one. The eyes of the painting were not on the original canvas but were on the leather flap instead. When the flap hung in place, which it usually did, the picture looked complete to the keenest observer who might happen to be in the saloon. When the flap was lifted, human eyes took the place of the painted eyes.

By this means Hoyt Durham could look into his barroom undetected and without leaving the office. Thus he could keep an eye on his trade, and on his employees, if need be. Curly Bottsinger used the device now to scan the big room. Gazing long and intently, he stiffened with excitement and straightened himself, his broad face twisting.

"It's him!" he said huskily. "He just walked into the place!"

"Who?" the third man demanded quickly.

"The new trouble-shooter. The one who

was confabbin' with Dan Callishaw at the hotel this morning. He's down below, I tell you! But that ain't all! I had a pretty fair look at that jigger this morning. But just for a minute as he stood inside the bat-wings, there was something about his face that — that — Hell, I would have swore he was Hellvation Hank McGrath, hisself!"

"Hellvation Hank," Hoyt Durham said emphatically, "is dead and buried!"

The third man crossed the room in two strides and crouched to have a look for himself. He came erect, his eyes narrowed thoughtfully. "He does look like Mc-Grath," he agreed. "I wonder —"

Curly Bottsinger was dragging a gun from its holster. "Hoyt, I'm going to plumb ruin your pretty pitcher," he snarled. "I'm guessin' that jigger maybe saw me around the Drovers' Rest this morning. I'm thinkin' he's come here lookin' for me! I'm going to drive a bullet right between the eyes of 'The Lady of the Nile' and likewise right between the eyes of that new trouble-shooter!"

"Wait, you fool!" snapped the third man, and his fingers closed on Bottsinger's wrist. "That won't do! There's half-a-hundred railroad workers down there lap-ping up whiskey. Supposing a man is murdered right before their eyes? They'll come stampeding up here and tear the place apart. I know the breed! Even if we slipped out before they got their hands on us, it wouldn't take Tyler Whitman ten minutes to add up things once he heard about it. He'd know The Three he talks about are using the Golden Slipper for their head-quarters. We can't risk that — yet. Things are touchy enough with a lot of people remembering that Hoyt, here, had a run-in with Hellvation Hank McGrath the same night that Hank died."

"But we can't let that jigger go snoopin' around here," Bottsinger argued frantically. "He's after me, I tell you! He must'a saw me!"

The eyes of the third man were dark with thought, and the other two turned silent at this sign of concentration, proof enough that he was the real leader there. At last the third man smiled. "I have it," he said. "I told you we'd let this new fellow alone for a while, unless opportunity laid him in our laps. I'm thinking it has — if we work it right. I've got a plan that will do the trick. Listen, gentlemen —"

6.

For a long time the Gospel Kid had stood in the musty room in the Drovers' Rest, looking upon the grotesquely sprawled body of Dan Callishaw. Then, knowing that life was forever gone from the man, he went downstairs. The clerk was again at his post at the desk, and to him the Kid spoke a few words, words that sent that worthy along the street to the undertaker's. The Kid's own footsteps took him back to the railroad's office, where he scribbled a few hasty words, handing the slip of paper to Key O'Dade.

"Since you had a message from Tyler Whitman this morning, I take it the wires are up across Crowfoot Gulch," said the Kid. "Can you get this through to Whitman?"

O'Dade read the message, a growing anger making his florid face redder than ever. "Dan Callishaw — dead!" he gasped. "So it's murderin' good men they've taken to doing! Bad cess to the three of them. Bad cess!"

"O'Dade," said the Kid, toying with a thought, "if you wanted to find the gun that shot Dan Callishaw, where would you start lookin'?"

Key O'Dade gave him a quick glance, running his stubby fingers through his red hair the while. "Faith and it's a riddle yez are askin' me, bhoy," he decided. "But it's the Golden Slipper Saloon where ye'll find gunmen hanging out, and it's Hoyt Durham that's hirin' thim kind o' gents these days. Just this mornin' two new ones drifted into town, askin' the way to that divil's own dance hall."

"The Golden Slipper, eh?" mused the Kid, and turned on his heel to go and seek the place.

He was playing a hunch, but there was no better way to pass the time until orders came from Tyler Whitman. Looking for the killer of Dan Callishaw in that teeming town would be like looking for a needle in a haystack — or worse, since he hadn't the faintest idea who might have triggered the murder gun. But there was always the chance that luck might favor a man, some odd clue come his way. That possibility, slender though it was, took the Kid through the batwings and into the glittering interior of the Golden Slipper.

Fifty-odd M.P. workers awaited the hour when the work train would pull out for end o' steel. Most of them were in this saloon, crowding the bar or milling in the gambling wing, a boisterous bunch who worked hard and played equally hard.

There were others there as well, gamblers and gunmen, and the Kid, standing in the doorway, had the sensation of eyes upon him. He'd known no presentiment of danger when he'd stood upon the edge of that doomed trestle the night before. But something prickled along his spine now, some vague warning, shapeless yet clamoring. But his darting glance saw nothing of hostility before him, so, ignoring a percentage girl who sidled toward him, he moved to the bar.

"Whiskey," he said.

But with the drink held significantly in his left hand, he left it untasted, toying idly with the glass. A great mirror, freighted in a decade before, ran the length of the wall behind the bar, doubling the battalion of bottles arrayed before it. In the polished glass, the Kid studied the place and the people who filled it. The paintings on the wall claimed his attention too, for he could see their reflections from where he stood. But it was the one called "The Lady of the

76

Nile" that really chained his eyes.

Just for an instant that picture had come to life! It was unbelievable — but it was so! For the space of a second there had been a subtle change in the lifeless canvas, a change the Kid discerned without being able to define it. His eyes glued to the picture's reflection, he watched it intently, hoping the change would come again; watched it in vain while the minutes dragged along in their endless march. He was still watching when a voice spoke at his elbow.

"Pretty, ain't she?"

The Kid glanced along his shoulder. The man who'd edged up to the bar beside him was as seedy a looking specimen as the Kid had ever seen — a gaunt, cadaverous creature with bleary eyes in a face that hadn't felt a razor for at least three days. Thin yellow hair, ragged and unkempt, fell to the collar of the corduroy coat the man wore, part of a suit that had obviously been slept in. The brand of a barfly was so plainly stamped on the fellow that the Kid anticipated his next remark before it was spoken.

"I'm down on my luck," the man whined in a nasal voice. "Could you buy a feller a drink?"

The Kid eyed him reflectively. "Been around here long?" he asked.

"Months now. Ever since last fall."

Brief as the answer was, it told the Kid what he wanted to know. He signaled a sweating bartender and ordered a bottle and a second glass. Wincing at the boom-town price he was forced to pay for the liquor, the Kid wondered if the investment would bring any worth-while returns. His guest slopped whiskey into the glass, and downed it in a single gulp. The Kid sipped his.

"Who," he asked, faint irony in his voice, "do I have the pleasure of drinking with?"

"Loomis. Shadow Loomis they call me. What difference does a name make?"

The Kid, who'd found it expedient to change his own name on occasion, had no answer for that one. This Loomis, he guessed, was probably some sort of remit-tance man, the blacksheep of a well-to-do Eastern family who'd shipped him to the frontier where his dissipations would reflect only upon himself. But because the Kid sensed that Loomis had once known a better life, he automatically responded to the demands of courtesy.

"McGrath is my name," he volunteered.

"McGrath?" Loomis turned it over on

78

his tongue. "There was another man here with that name."

"I know," the Kid prompted him. "He was murdered last fall."

Shadow Loomis poured himself another drink without waiting for an invitation. "He shouldn't have opened the door without a gun," he observed morosely. "He shouldn't have left the light at his back to make a target out of himself. He should have known better than to take such a chance."

The Kid felt the swift urge of excitement but made sure that his voice betrayed none of it. "What do you know about that?" he asked easily. "How do you know he opened the door without a gun?"

Shadow Loomis shrugged.

"How does anybody know? He was found dead in front of his own shack, and there was no gun on him." His voice faltered, and his eyes roved around the room as though in search of something to anchor his thoughts. "A pretty picture there on the wall, eh?" he observed. " 'The Lady of the Nile' they call her. She can see, friend; and she can hear. And some day she'll speak. You mark my word and don't forget it. Just remember that Shadow Loomis told you."

The Kid looked at Loomis in disgust as

the barfly poured another drink. The man was crazy, the Kid decided, or at least so addle-witted from too much alcohol as to be hardly worth bothering with. Certainly his mouthings were meaningless gibberish. But as the Kid shifted his gaze to the mirror, studying the man in the polished depths, his own eyes narrowed thoughtfully. Suddenly he wasn't so sure that he had correctly gauged this Shadow Loomis.

"You're kin to Hellvation Hank?" Shadow Loomis asked, dragging a sleeve across his mouth.

Before the Kid could answer, that presentiment of danger throbbed through him again, clamoring and persistent. But the warning bell tolled too late, for suddenly danger was an actuality rather than a shadowy foreboding.

The whole thing happened mighty fast. A man had crowded to the bar beside the Kid, a tall, angular man, beard-stubbled and loose-lipped. Dusty range garb clothed him, but he wore his guns too low to be a cowboy. "Give a feller elbow room, can't yuh!" the man growled, and shouldered the Kid away so violently as to send him staggering backward to crash against a second man who stood a pace away from the bar, almost directly behind the Kid.

This other fellow, barrel-like in build, a swarthy-faced man with close-set eyes, cursed him viciously. "Watch where yuh're goin'!" he snarled, and shoved the Kid, hurling him back against the first man.

The play was so well timed, so patently a planned job of trouble-making that it shrieked a warning to the Kid. The anger that blazed in the eyes of both these men was completely out of proportion to the thing that prompted it, while the tied-down holsters of the two proclaimed their calling — and their intent. Professional gun-hands!

Others saw the play and read its portent. First there was a doomsday hush in the saloon. Then came general bedlam as men suddenly fell over each other in a mad scramble to get out of the possible line of fire.

Shadow Loomis had slid away as silently as though he were made of the substance of his sobriquet. The Kid stood alone with the two men on either side of him. In this way he was at an angle where they could catch him in a raking crossfire once they went for their guns. And that's what they were going to do — just as soon as the situation built a halfway plausible excuse for them.

The Kid gave each of them a look. *"Get at it!"* he said with a vast disgust.

They needed no further invitation. The Kid was facing the taller of the two. He didn't need to see the man's downward darting hand, for the gesture registered in the fellow's yellowish eyes. Instantly the Kid was twisting aside, jerking his own gun in the same motion, bringing it up flaming. The walls sent back hammering echoes as two guns roared, and the Kid fell sideways to the floor. The tall gunman fell too, drilled through the heart.

But only one dead man sprawled upon the floor. The tall gunman's bullet had breathed hotly past the Kid's ear, missing him by a narrow margin. He had purposely fallen to save himself from the second gunman, the one he hadn't been able to watch. And the ruse had worked, for a bullet droned over his head as he fell. Hitting the floor, the Kid rolled, a second shot from the squat gunman geysering dust into his eyes. It was touch-and-go for a moment. But firing from the floor, the Kid saw the man bow before him, take three hesitant steps, then trip over his partner to fall dead on top of the taller man. It was over as quickly as that.

The Kid came to his feet, his gun still in

his hand, his eyes flicking from one face to another, measuring the men who crowded against the far wall.

"Which one of you is Hoyt Durham?" he demanded, his face bleak, his voice like a clarion in the hush that held the crowd.

Any one of the posts that supported the ceiling was thick enough to keep bullets from reaching a man. From the shelter of one of these posts Hoyt Durham stepped, his swarthy face as expressionless as the top of a table. "I'm Durham, stranger," he said. "Some mighty nice shooting you did. What can I do for you?"

"These your men?"

Durham stroked his skimpy moustache, his gaze sliding over the two dead gunmen. "They wanted to be," he said. "They came here this morning, asking for a job. A man in my position sometimes has to have others to guard his back, but I have no use for professional killers of their stripe. They expected to find an easy meal-ticket, but I turned them down. That's what put them on the prod, probably."

Stooping, the Kid turned one of the dead gunmen's pockets inside out. A handful of gold coins tinkled to the floor. The Kid scattered them with the toe of his boot, sending them rolling every direction, as he straightened.

"Probably!" he mocked.

His gaze locked with Hoyt Durham's, and in that instant a name drummed persistently through the Kid's head. *Herod!* A red-handed king who had lesser men do his killing for him. But there wasn't a shred of proof to back his suspicions. Therefore he pouched his gun, and his exposed back was eloquent of his contempt as he strode across the floor and out of the saloon without another word.

His footsteps had no purpose as he shouldered along the crowded walk, a reckless anger burning within him. But its aftermath was saner thought, born of a summary of what had happened. He had brushed with death and come through unscathed, but that was not the significant thing. That play in the Golden Slipper proved that he was marked for destruction, even as Dan Callishaw had been marked, and he had to walk with danger from then on.

Which meant that The Three knew him for what he was and feared him — either as Hellvation Hank's brother or as the trouble-shooter for the Montana-Pacific. He wondered how they had managed to identify him so quickly. And because there was only one solution, he knew that the killer of Dan Callishaw must have been skulking in the hotel hallway when he, the Kid, had announced himself to Callishaw.

He was recalling that talk with Callishaw — and its aftermath — when he found himself abreast of a building whose big bay window bore the lettering: CAPROCK TRIBUNE — THACKERY WEAVER, EDITOR, and he turned inside.

Enthroned behind a huge pigeonholed desk in a littered room, rank with the odor of ink and glue, sat a plump, pink-cheeked, gray-headed man who blinked at the Kid owlishly through a pair of thick glasses. A frock coat and a flowing tie gave to the man a dignity which was entirely out of keeping with his slovenly establishment.

"You Weaver?" the Kid asked.

"I'm Thackery Weaver," the man admitted. "Can I be of service to you?"

"You can answer a question," said the Kid. "You gave Dan Callishaw a write-up in your paper, a write-up that mentioned everything about him, includin' the date of his birth. Do you always make it a point to find out a man's birthday?"

Thackery Weaver beamed pridefully. "The Caprock *Tribune* boasts of its thorough-ness," he said grandiloquently. "In these stirring days we find it pays to be alert. In our files we have complete lists of data on anybody of importance. Should a piece of news break, we can instantly embellish it with all the necessary details."

"I savvy," the Kid said stonily. "You could practically write your obituaries ahead of time. You've got a finger on everybody in town, eh?"

"Anybody who is prominent," the editor assured him. "I can supply the date of birth, the place, the past history of all our leading citizens, including newcomers like Tyler Whitman and Kurt Ormond and —"

"I'd like to have a look at those lists," the Kid interjected.

Thackery Weaver came out of his chair. Standing, he proved to be short and pudgy, and if he hoped to look belligerent he only looked ludicrous. "Just who are you, mister?" he demanded in a less cordial tone.

"Trouble-shooter for the Montana-Pacific," the Kid said. "Now trot out those lists. I crave to see just who's included in them."

Weaver hesitated, shrugged his shoulders, and moved over to an old-fashioned filing cabinet standing against one ink-smudged wall. Dragging out a drawer, he fumbled in its depths for several minutes, his search growing more frantic as it produced no visible results. When he turned, his pink jowls sagged with amazement.

"They're gone!" he cried. "My lists are gone — stolen! What do you know about this, mister? What made you so interested in them?"

"Never mind," said the Kid. He was studying the little newspaper man, trying to read Thackery Weaver's character and to fit it into one of three patterns. But Weaver was a hard man to read. Those glasses made him so, for they distorted his appearance.

"What do you think about the railroad?" the Kid asked casually. "Any good reason why it shouldn't run through this section?"

"The railroad?" Weaver repeated, and instantly struck a pose. "The railroad is the dream of every far-sighted citizen of Caprock, and our paper was the first to point out the benefits to come from such an undertaking. Why, in an early editorial of mine — But wait, I have a clipping in my files. I'll read it to you —"

"Don't bother," the Kid said brusquely, then softened his tone. "I'm thankin' you for your trouble. And here's a tip for you. There's big news for your paper at the

Drovers' Rest and at the Golden Slipper Saloon today. Better go after it pronto."

Weaver reached for paper and pencil. "News!" he cried excitedly. "But you're news too, if you're an M.P. trouble-shooter. I'd like to give you a write-up in the paper. Now if you'll just give me some data such as —"

"No thanks," the Kid said drily. "I'm the shyest damn violet that ever bloomed, Weaver."

Leaving the place, he went to the railroad office where he found a telegram waiting for him. Tyler Whitman's name was at the bottom of the message, and the briefness of the wire was characteristic of the railroad builder.

"SORRY ABOUT CALLISHAW," it read. "YOU ARE PROMOTED. REPORT TO ORMOND."

The work train was chugging out of Caprock, and the Kid made it on the run. He found a seat in a car overcrowded with graders and steel-layers and, hunkering there, gave himself to reflection, the events of this exciting day parading through his mind.

It was only then that he recalled something he'd completely forgotten in the excitement of the gun-duel in the saloon and the meeting with Thackery Weaver afterwards. Shadow Loomis. . . .

That mysterious man might be a piece to the puzzle, too. Loomis was seemingly a dissolute barfly, a man who'd sell his soul for a shot of whiskey. Yet he didn't play the part to perfection. Watching him in the mirror, the Kid had seen Loomis step out of character once, but the Kid hadn't had a chance to do anything about the discovery, for the trouble had commenced almost instantly afterwards.

None of which changed the facts. Shadow Loomis had begged for liquor and downed his first drink. The Kid wasn't so sure about the others. But one thing was certain — Shadow Loomis had poured his last drink into the cuspidor at his feet. For Matt McGrath had seen him do it.

7.

The Gospel Kid was always to remember his first glimpse of end o' steel.

He reached it in the late afternoon when the prairie lay golden beneath the dying sun, and the marching shadows filled the draws with flowing darkness. With his neck craned from a window of the work train, he had his initial look at what was to be a familiar scene in the days to come. Beyond Caprock the rails had reached to reach no farther, their jerky march to the mountains halted by the icy hand of a Montana winter. But now the Montana-Pacific was stirring to activity like a hibernating bear freshly released from its season of bondage.

Weatherbeaten tents and construction shacks, a colorless sea of them, mottled the prairie. Supplies were scattered everywhere. The bridge crews were a score of miles ahead, and, beyond them, a tunnel crew was already drilling a hole through the first barrier of the lofty Big Thunders. But most of the workers were there, a teeming army of them who swarmed along the welt of the grade where loose ties lay scattered, and the clang of sledge against spike blended with the hissing of a locomotive, the hoarse voices of teamsters urging work horses to a greater effort — a medley of sound that was the tuneless song of construction. It was chaos, set to a pattern. It was confusion, dedicated to a driving purpose.

In one shack a telegraph instrument clacked ceaselessly, and nearby, standing on a siding, was a special car with a lonely sort of dignity to it — the office of the engineering staff. A brawny worker pointed it out to the Kid, and he crossed to it after he had stood gazing at the scene before him for a long time. In the car he found Kurt Ormond busy at a desk piled high with reports and papers.

Waiting for the moment when Ormond would be free, the Kid studied this man who was second in command to Tyler Whitman. He was surprised to see that Ormond was apparently little older than thirty — a still-faced, sharp-featured man, browned by exposure. He wore boots and breeches now, and a white shirt, open at the throat, and this garb befitted him more than the broadcloth that had been his

91

apparel when he'd visited Caprock the previous fall. Yet there was something about Ormond to indicate that he would be as much at home in an Eastern drawing room as here on the edge of the raw frontier.

The Kid wasn't sure whether he liked Ormond or not. The chief engineer had a machine-like quality about him that made him as impersonal as a donkey-engine. When he turned to speak, that quality was emphasized by his brisk, metallic voice.

"Well?" the engineer asked.

"Whitman told me to report to you," the Kid explained. "I'm McGrath, the new trouble-shooter. Dan Callishaw won't be out here. He's dead."

Ormond settled back in his chair, clasping his hands behind his head. "I know," he said. "I was in Caprock and came out on the special, just ahead of the work train. Thackery Weaver couldn't wait to go to press with the news; he was playing town crier and shouting about what had happened to Dan. But never mind that. If Whitman hired you — you're working for M.P. But I'm not so sure it was a good idea."

The Kid chose a chair and folded his lanky body to accommodate himself to it. "You don't like my looks, eh?" he guessed.

"I've nothing personal against you," Ormond said. "I just happen to know a lot about you. The queer thing is that Ty knows those same things and hired you anyway. You see, your brother and Whitman were old friends. Hellvation Hank was a man in anybody's language, but you're a different kind of gent. Now don't get your tail-feathers ruffled! I don't mean to say you're not a fighter."

"I'm not gettin' mad," the Kid said mildly. "I'm just gettin' interested."

"You were mixed up in a few shady deals down in Texas, McGrath. You know it, and we know it, so there's no use arguing about that. Besides, your back-trail makes no difference to me — so long as you play square with Montana-Pacific. But I'm wondering. At a time when the road is fighting for its very life, and when the Eastern investors who are backing us are wondering if they've poured their money down a prairie-dog hole, I'm not so sure I want a man around whose history has as many missing pages as yours, McGrath. Do we understand each other?"

"I reckon," the Kid said without rancor. "Anything else?"

"You're here to avenge your brother," Ormond went on. "I can read that in your eyes. It would please M.P. mightily if you caught up with The Three. But the fact remains that the railroad comes first, so long as you're working for us. Maybe you'll be off riding your own trail just when we need you the worst."

The Kid caressed his rocky jaw and smiled mirthlessly.

"Me, I've got two jobs to do," he said. "One of them is to see Montana-Pacific steel cross the Big Thunders. That would be a sort of monument for Hank — but maybe you wouldn't understand about that. If I have to do any other chore first, I'll quit the railroad. Right now I crave to go to work. Callishaw said something about an agitator being out here. Maybe I should have a look-see around."

Ormond nodded. "Somebody's stirring up the crews," he admitted. "I've never been able to put my finger on the right man, but I haven't had time to really try and smoke him out. Some of the work is let out on contract, with the contractors supplying their own men. That means there are a lot of strange faces around camp. Go have a look — but be careful."

The Kid unlimbered himself from the chair but paused at the door. "Met a queer gent in Caprock today," he said. "Shadow

Loomis he calls himself. Know him?"

Ormond's interest quickened. "I know him," he said. "Looks like a barfly, but I've wondered about him. I'd like a line on him, McGrath. If you get the chance, have a talk with him and see what you can find out."

The Kid nodded, and the moment he stepped from the car Kurt Ormond was out of his mind. The engineer had been blunt, outspoken, but the Kid packed no grudge on that score. They were part of Montana-Pacific, the two of them, each with a job to do. Part of Ormond's job had been to weigh Matt McGrath, give him the acid test for any weakness he might find. That was as it should be, the Kid decided. And his own job was just as clear-cut.

Blending with the toiling crews, the Kid made an unobtrusive tour of inspection, seeing men who worked hard and men who worked lazily and studying all of them in silence. There was a certain advantage in the fact that he was new there — an advantage which neither Dan Callishaw nor Kurt Ormond had enjoyed. He wasn't recognized as a railroad man, so his presence didn't spur the lazy to a pretense of industry. But the Kid wasn't concerned with lazy men — it was something sinister he sought. And within an hour he found it.

Far out on the grade, a crew of a score of men leveled the roadbed, their pace determining the pace of those who came behind them — the sweating track-layers and those husky, bare-armed men who swung the sledges to inch the rails toward the west. Here was the key to the trouble that slowed down the Montana-Pacific. Watching the outfit, the Kid saw them loitering along, putting their heads together for whispered consultations time and again, while those behind had to wait for them to proceed.

The straw-boss of this sluggish crew was a big man, a broad-shouldered giant who'd been on the work train out of Caprock. The Kid had paid little attention to him on the trip, but now he sized up the man purposefully. A pretty big mouthful for a fellow the size of himself to chew, he decided. Yet he tapped the giant's shoulder.

"Me, I'd like to talk to you," he said.

The giant turned, and for an instant he stood slack-jawed, his eyes widening. Then his self-confidence returned and his lips curled as he surveyed the Kid from head to foot, with calculating appraisal.

"Texas man, eh?" he said. "I saw you in the Golden Slipper today. You're mighty handy with your gun, but I never knew a

Tejano yet that was worth two cents without his cutter. I got nothing to talk about with you. Get out o' here, mister, before you get tramped on!"

The Kid smiled. From the corner of his eye he saw Kurt Ormond striding toward them, and he waited for the chief engineer's arrival. "Stick around, Ormond," the Kid advised. "I've found the gent we was talking about, I'm thinkin'. Here's where I start earning my pay."

"You're crazy!" Ormond whispered as the Kid slipped off his gun-belt. "It's Curly Bottsinger you're bucking! Even if you're sure you're right, you'd better let me find a way to handle him. He's the toughest rough-and-tumble man in the Caprocks. Do you want to get killed?"

"Shucks," said the Kid. "The Caprocks ain't so big. You ought to see the size of the Panhandle, Ormond."

He hit Bottsinger then. His left fist arced to smash bunched knuckles into the giant's face, a terrific blow.

"Get at it!" the Kid said with a vast disgust.

It was the quickest way to get things started, the Kid had decided, for the problem had resolved itself into very simple terms. He'd found the man who was delaying the steel. That man was the kind who could understand no argument but action. Therefore Matt McGrath would talk to this man in his own language.

But the blow scarcely shook Bottsinger. He came forward with a wild rush, and the Kid was cold with the realization that it had been a great deal easier to start this fight than it was going to be to finish it.

Bottsinger's fists lashed out over the Kid's head as the Texan bobbed beneath them. For a single second the giant was off balance. In that golden moment the Kid's right whammed against Bottsinger's chin. There was a lot of steel in the Kid's lanky length, and most of it was behind his fist. But the giant only laughed at the blow, his own fist swinging. The Kid saw it coming — saw it too late. He tried to twist aside, but Bottsinger's knuckles grazed his shoulder, sending the Kid somersaulting backwards upon the ground.

With a roar of triumph, Bottsinger came after him, and the giant's intent was obvious. It was going to be a rough-and-tumble fight now, the kind of fight where the immense bulk of Bottsinger would be an overwhelming advantage. But as the giant launched himself upon the fallen

Texan, Matt rolled to his back and his legs jackknifed, his boots crashing against Bottsinger's broad chest, hurling the man away. Before Bottsinger could recover himself to rush again, the Kid was on his feet and carrying the fight to him, his arms pistoning.

They crashed together, slugging toe to toe, ruthless, smashing blows, until the Kid turned himself into a dancing, darting figure — hard to find and harder to hit. All the while his own fists were taking toll of the giant. Cheers went up, for the Montana-Pacific had suddenly declared an unofficial recess, and every worker ringed the fighters in a yelling, excited circle, shouting advice that was only a dull roar in the ears of the Kid.

It was a battle that was to go down in the annals of the Montana-Pacific, and at first the Kid was sick with the thought that its end was inevitable defeat for himself. He had tackled Bottsinger because it was part of his job, but there was another reason as well.

Kurt Ormond had been dubious about the Kid — and not entirely without justification. Possibly Tyler Whitman had had his misgivings as well, in spite of the fact that the railroad builder had hired him without hesitation. Here was the chance to prove himself to both of them, he thought. Then he wondered once again if he'd bitten off a great deal more than he was going to be able to chew.

But he was still on his feet, still slugging, and it came to him that he'd worn the fine edge from the fighting strength of Curly Bottsinger. True, the man was still before him, a red, blurry shadow that refused to go down. But Bottsinger's blows had less dynamite behind them. The Kid threw himself into the fray with a fresh fervor, born of the first faint glimmer of hope.

Like a devil let loose, he ripped rights and lefts to Bottsinger's body and face, taking punishment the while, yet dodging the giant's mallet-like fists time and again with an automatic efficiency. Once they went down together, Bottsinger's thumb fumbling for the Kid's eyes. But the Kid managed to heave him aside, come erect again, and the giant came after him. Then it was an endless repetition of a thing that had become a nightmare — slug and dodge, hit and ride with a blow, drive and drive and drive until that bloody bulk before him was no more.

He had only the haziest notion how long they'd been fighting. He was like a man in a troubled dream whose motions are sluggish when speed is needed, whose strength is water when it has to be steel. He feinted awkwardly, his gesture threatening Bottsinger's midriff. The giant dropped his huge fists for protection, and his massive jaw was exposed. The Kid had hit that jaw a dozen times before, but he hit it again, hit it with everything he had left. Bottsinger fell, sprawling loosely on the ground.

The Kid stared at him, bleary-eyed. Bottsinger would be up again. He'd be back with those merciless fists flailing. And when he came this time, the Kid would go down. He knew that. He could gauge his own powers, and he'd gone to their very limit. But something was decidedly wrong, for Bottsinger wasn't getting up. Bottsinger was staying on the ground.

Spitting out a tooth, the giant forced a single muttered word through his broken lips: "Enough. . . ."

Bottsinger was beaten! And horny hands were seizing the Kid, for the circle of spectators had broken and a hundred men were surrounding him, pounding his back, trying to shake his hand. But there was strength enough in the Kid to speak, and he did, his voice sounding nothing like his own.

"Gents," he said, "I'm no great shakes with a shovel or a sledge, but I'd shore like to see this road finished. I reckon you'll have to do the rest of it. Back to it, you terriers!"

They were a fighting breed, these workers, and they could understand the language of a fighting man. They returned to the grade enthusiastically, and only the Kid, weak and dizzy, stood there with Kurt Ormond. Bottsinger painfully propped himself upon one elbow.

"You're a McGrath all right, damn you!" the giant snarled. "Hellvation Hank was the only man your size who ever packed your kind of wallop!"

"Get out when you're able!" the Kid said wearily. "Get out — and stay out!"

"God!" Ormond ejaculated, and there was admiration intermingled with astonishment in the engineer's eyes. "You just manhandled the giant of the Caprock country."

"A giant?" the Kid repeated, and shook his head. " 'And there went out a champion out of the camp of the Philistines,' " he muttered, " 'named Goliath of Gath. . . .' "

"What's that?" Ormond asked.

But the Kid made no answer, for it was

102

only a hunch he had. But there was balm for his bruised body in the thought that perhaps he'd just met up with another of The Three — and beaten the man.

To the west, the sun was slipping behind the Big Thunders. This day was nearly done, and soon flares would be lighted so that the night crews could work. A good day, the Kid reflected. He'd done his share of work, and he looked forward to rest. He began limping toward the car that was the office of the engineering staff, with Kurt Ormond steadying him. But halfway there they were halted by the telegrapher, who darted from his shack, a slip of paper in his hand. He thrust it at Ormond, whose jaw went tight as he read it.

"Bad news?" the Kid asked, and a premonition told him that the day's work was not yet finished.

"Read it," Ormond urged, and handed the slip to the Kid. It was addressed to Ormond, and Tyler Whitman's name was at its bottom, and it told a man all he needed to know.

"RIFLEMEN IN CROWFOOT GULCH PICKING OFF CLEAN-UP CREW REPAIRING TRESTLE," it read. "IMPOSSIBLE TO FINISH WORK HERE UNLESS THEY ARE ROUTED.

COME AT ONCE, AND BRING AS
MANY FIGHTING MEN AS YOU CAN
POSSIBLY SPARE."

8.

Riflemen in Crowfoot Gulch! The forces who harassed the Montana-Pacific Railroad had struck again, were making another attempt to sever the artery that fed life-blood to the end of steel.

There was very little that Matt McGrath knew of railroading. But he could reason, even as The Three had reasoned when they'd planned this move in the little room in Hoyt Durham's Golden Slipper, and the Kid knew that calamity had come. If that trestle wasn't repaired, the work there would cease just as surely as though every brawny track-layer had thrown down his tools and called quits.

It was a situation that called for immediate action, and the challenge of it was enough to slough some of the Kid's weariness away. He was astonished that Kurt Ormond still stood here, the telegram in his hand, his inscrutable face furrowed with thought.

"How many fighting men can you spare away from camp?" the Kid asked.

"It isn't that," Ormond said. "It's just that I'm wondering — This business at Crowfoot doesn't make sense. Supposing raiders are making it hot for the clean-up crew? Surely those marauders know they can't hold out forever, keep the trestle from being repaired. Are they going to all this bother just to make a few hours' delay? McGrath, I'm thinking the whole thing is a ruse, a plan to draw most of us away from end o' steel, leaving this camp unprotected!"

The Kid turned the argument over in his mind and had to admit the logic of it. But: "Tyler Whitman's running this road, isn't he?" he asked. "He's told us to come. Ormond, there're times when a man can be too cautious."

The chief engineer took the rebuke without coloring, but for a moment the eyes of the two were locked. And in that moment they were two men, each with the iron to rule, each with a purpose. But it was Ormond who broke under the Kid's eyes.

"You're right, McGrath," he conceded, and the Kid was to remember that he had never admired Kurt Ormond so much as at that moment. "I'll order the work train and one coach around. About twenty picked men is all we should need. That'll leave enough here to keep an eye on things if anyone should strike at this camp. But you — you're in no shape to do any more today. You don't have to come along unless you want to, McGrath."

"Thanks," the Kid said. "But me, I reckon I'll just string along."

And he did, piling into the coach while Ormond drew himself into the cab of the locomotive after guns had been issued to a selected score of workers. These men, accepting the assignment as though it were in the nature of a holiday, were soon aboard the train.

There was all the confusion of getting under way and, after that, a wild ride across the unleveled rails with pistons screaming and drivers pounding. Caprock lay many miles to the east, but each of those miles was covered in less than two minutes. The Kid was grateful for this interlude of inactivity, using the minutes to soak up rest and recuperate from the punishment Curly Bottsinger had dealt him.

Dusk was a gray mantle over Caprock, and the town was throbbing with the first phase of its boisterous night life, when they flashed through it. Beyond Caprock the Kid dozed, only to be jerked awake when the engine finally wheezed to a stop. When he swung from the coach along with the score of fighting men, he discovered that it was now quite dark. But there was light enough in the scene before them.

The work train stood on the west bank of Crowfoot Gulch, facing east, and across the gulch another work train faced it, the glow from the two head lamps bathing the trestle in brilliancy. Over on the other side of the gulch, a cluster of men standing near the other train were shadowy and shapeless. The gulch was a yawning void of darkness, and so hush-filled as to give the lie to the summons that had brought them there.

Yet the Kid wasn't fooled. The place was crawling with death, and the chill of it was in the air. The quiet was an ominous quiet, freighted with portent. Ormond seemed to sense it too as he joined the Kid. The chief engineer shivered involuntarily, and his eyes were everywhere as he probed the veiling shadows beyond the light.

"Whitman!" he called. "You over there?"

The yonder darkness found voice. "Here, Ormond. Those gunmen are down in the gulch. Be careful, man. They'll start shooting the minute any of us show ourselves."

Ormond bit his lip and glanced toward the Kid. "This is more in your line, McGrath," he admitted. "What do you suggest we do?"

"You've got to use bait to catch yourself a bunch of coyotes," the Kid decided, after due reflection. "Supposing you keep half our men, Ormond. Move northward along this rim of the gulch. I'll take the other half and cross the trestle. Looks like it's repaired enough to hold our weight, even if it won't carry a train. Me and my boys'll Injun up the other side of the gulch."

"Catch 'em between the two outfits," Ormond said.

The Kid nodded. "I thought I saw something stirring yonder, north of the trestle. Ty Whitman can start a little activity here at the trestle. When the guns start spitting down below, we'll know for sure where those raiders are hunkerin'. Tell your men to mark the gunflashes and make their own bullets count. Once we get them hellions on the run, we can work down into the gulch and really rout 'em. But when you come into the gulch, watch out for me and my men, because we'll be working down from the opposite side."

"Good enough," Ormond nodded, and tolled off ten of the men.

"Douse that light!" the Kid ordered the engineer of the work train, and called a like order across the gulch. Then there was darkness, complete and enveloping, with only the steel rails shining in the first faint starlight.

"Ready?" the Kid asked, and his men nodded.

He edged out upon the trestle, the ten strung out behind him. For the first few moments the silence held. Then the darkness below was bristling with gunflame, and lead sleeted in their midst. The Kid's gun flung back a fiery reply, and others behind him answered bullets with bullets. But they were exposed and at a tremendous disadvantage, and the Kid did not tarry to make war under such circumstances. With a brusque, "Come on!" he was sprinting to the east end of the trestle, his men pounding after him.

They made it unscathed, and on the other side the Kid hastily outlined his plan to Whitman, who nodded his approval. "Leave the lights off," the Kid said, "and just stir up enough fuss to draw their fire. Meanwhile me and Ormond will be getting into position."

"Be careful!" Whitman warned him.

"I will," the Kid promised, and saw,

then, one form, slighter than the others, standing well in the background.

Somehow he hadn't thought of Tara Herndon still being there. He knew that no train could cross the gulch and get on into Caprock until the trestle was repaired, but he'd presumed that arrangements had been made to get the passengers onward by other means. He'd forgotten that there hadn't been time for that, for the swift pace of the day's events had made the past twenty hours seem like so many days to him.

The passenger train that he'd stopped the night before had been backed to division headquarters, at Rimrock, just that side of the Dakota border. With the work train that had been sent out from Rimrock, there'd also been a coach. Tara Herndon had spent the day enthralled by the spectacle of men doing a month's work in the span of a few hours. When the bullets had begun to burn she'd been ordered inside a coach by Whitman, along with the few other passengers, but the lull had brought her forth again.

But the Kid gave her no more than a glance and a nod, for there was work to be done. He was about to start off when a young, yellow-haired man in boots and breeches plucked at his sleeve.

"I'd like to come along with you," the fellow said. "I've been itching to get close enough to those devils to use a gun on them."

The Kid remembered this youngster, and remembered Whitman saying, the night before, "You, Hanson! There's an emergency telegraph lay-out in the tool shack back a piece."

"O.K., Hanson," the Kid decided.

Once the shadows had swallowed them, the Kid became tight-lipped and wary, moving as silently as he could, his men imitating him. He had proceeded two hundred yards along the gulch's rim before there was a faint stirring on the trestle behind them. That would be Whitman, carrying out his part of the plan. Then, down below, rifles started yammering again.

Scorning silence now, the Kid picked a gunflash, aimed deliberately, and his barking gun wrung almost a dozen echoes from his companions' weapons. Across the gulch, flame lashed downward too, evidence enough that Ormond's crew had stationed themselves and were taking a hand.

They'd caught the renegades in a crossfire, and startled curses evidenced the efficiency of the Kid's strategy. They'd been having a high time of it, those skulkers of the darkness, hunkering in concealment and peppering away at toiling trestle builders. This was quite another proposition. But they were quick enough to swivel their guns, for suddenly bullets were clipping the bushes about the Kid and his men, and lead was ricocheting from the rocks, singing a sad, wailing song.

There were no more than half a dozen men below, the Kid guessed. He wondered if one of them was the oldster he'd tackled on the ledge the night before. But such thoughts were secondary, for most of his faculties were concentrated on the grim job of marking a target, loosing lead at it, loading, marking another target — an endless routine.

At last the break came, manifesting itself in a lessening of the gunfire below and a shifting of positions which was betrayed by the spearheads of flame. The raiders were gradually retreating up the coulee, giving way before those barrages from the rims. And the Kid, sensing that a complete rout might be a matter of minutes, knew it was time to carry the fight to the enemy if it was ever to be done.

His whispered command was passed

along the line. Then Matt McGrath was plunging down the coulee's side, threshing through the bushes, rolling and stumbling and coming to his feet again. From the far side of the gulch there was a similar commotion. Ormond and his crew were closing in!

If luck had favored them, they might have caught the raiders between the closing jaws of a trap. But the noise made by their descent was warning enough. Above the crashing of bushes in the gulch's bottom, there came the creak of saddle leather, the startled shouts of men, the ring of steel upon stone. Those sounds told the Kid that here was a factor which was going to count against his plan. The raiders had horses and were hitting the saddles. Once mounted, there would be no capturing them, since the railroaders were afoot.

The coulee's bottom was a pool of darkness at first. But the moon was edging over the eastern horizon now, and the Kid's eyes had become accustomed to the night while he'd hunkered on the rim. Thus he saw one man, slower than the others, swinging astride his horse. With a wild shout the Kid sprinted toward him, and at his side was the young engineer, Hanson.

"Stop!" Hanson cried, and it was the last

thing he ever said.

The renegade had rammed his rifle into its saddle sheath. But he snatched at his six-gun in the act of mounting, and it spat viciously. Beside the Kid, Hanson stumbled and went down, moaning once and no more. But something in the sound of it wrung all the caution out of Matt McGrath. Leaping forward, he was upon the renegade instantly. The fellow's gun barked again, the bullet burning through the Kid's clothes. Then the Kid had pinned the fellow upon the ground, and the renegade went limp beneath his hands.

The other M.P. fighters were hustling up, the forces from both rims merging at that spot. Kurt Ormond, a smoking gun clutched in his hand, came panting. "Get one of 'em?" he barked.

"Just one," the Kid said. "Look to Hanson. I think he's dead."

Ormond bent, fumbled with the engineer's shirt-front, and nodded significantly as he came to his feet.

"They've slipped away from us, the rest of them," the Kid observed angrily. "It would be a fool's chase to take the trail afoot. Besides, they could ambush us further up the coulee easy enough. I think they've had their belly-full for tonight, and there'll be no more trouble in Crowfoot Gulch. We'll tote this skunk back to Whitman. Some of you boys lend a hand and fetch Hanson."

Getting the dead man and the groggy prisoner up the slope to the coulee's east rim was a task. But they found a trail of sorts, and at last the ascent was finished and they were prodding the renegade on toward the dim outlines of the locomotive and the group who waited there. Ormond made his report to his superior, and it was brief enough.

"Hanson dead!" Tyler Whitman said hoarsely, and his fingers faltered to his forehead. Then: "Let's see what this prisoner has to say for himself." He faced the man, his voice even enough. "Who are you working for?" Whitman demanded. "Who hired you to bedevil us?"

The prisoner had recovered his senses and a belligerent contempt along with them. He was a big-bodied man with the flat, expressionless face of a stone idol, and viciousness had left a stamp upon him that nothing could ever eradicate. He hitched his belt and spat at Whitman's boot toe.

"You'd like tuh know, wouldn't you?" he jeered. "But you ain't ever gonna!"

It was obvious that Whitman bridled his

116

temper with an effort. "I don't know what else you've done, stranger," he said. "But you killed a mighty fine boy tonight — a boy who had a lot of good years ahead of him. Do you know what you've got coming for that?"

"Nothing," the man retorted insolently. "Where's the law that's gonna punish me?"

Tyler Whitman fell silent before that challenge, and the Kid jogged his elbow.

"Is he tellin' it straight?" the Kid demanded.

Whitman nodded. "I'm afraid so. There's a town marshal in Caprock — an old fellow who has never had anything more dangerous to do than jail a drunken cowpoke on pay night. He'll beg out by maintaining that since this happened outside Caprock, it doesn't come under his jurisdiction. The territorial pen is a long ways off, and it's just about as far to Fort Yellowstone and military law."

"In Texas, there's a law called rope law," the Kid said grimly. "It comes in mighty handy when regular law ain't around to take care of gents like this one."

"You mean — ?"

"We've got a rope, ain't we?" the Kid went on. "And there's a trestle to hang him from — the same trestle that was dynamited by him, or others like him, last night."

Whitman's eyes flitted to where the silent form of Hanson lay stretched upon the ground, a blanket tossed over it. "Maybe you're right," he said.

But Kurt Ormond stared aghast. "Whitman, have you lost your senses?" he demanded. "We can't take the law into our own hands like this! It isn't right from any standpoint, and it will give us a black eye back East. What about our promoters who are trying to raise more capital for the road? What are they going to be able to say when the word goes out that M.P. is running roughshod out here in Montana, taking the law into its hands, killing off men who stand in the way?"

"Hanson's got kinfolks, probably," the Kid said quietly. "Do you want the chore of writing to them, telling them what happened to him, Ormond?"

It stopped Ormond, that question, and it turned the face of Tyler Whitman to stone. The prisoner was paler now, some of his swagger gone, but arrogance still perched on his shoulders and contempt still glittered in his eyes. Then, in the doomsday hush, Tara burst suddenly into the midst of the men. But the storm of her fury broke about the head of the Gospel Kid only.

"So it's a hanging you want!" she raged. "You — You — ! By what right do *you*, of all people, set yourself up as judge, jury, and executioner of another man? Do you think that none of us here know how you came by your knowledge of rope law? Doesn't that Bible you carry have anything to say about, 'Let he who is without sin among you cast the first stone'?"

The Kid couldn't know how completely savage he looked to her, with his lips puffed and discolored by his fight with Bottsinger, and one eye nearly swelled shut. But his voice was soft enough, and there was no rebuke in it.

"Yes," he said. "The Book has them words. And it also has something to say about 'an eye for an eye, a tooth for a tooth.'"

"You don't fool me with your garbled quotations, McGrath!" Ormond suddenly snarled. "You figure this fellow works for The Three, and you'll enjoy seeing him dangle for that reason. It's the very thing I warned you about this afternoon! You're putting personal interests ahead of the road!"

One stride brought the Kid before

119

Ormond, and his hand closed on the engineer's shirt-front. "You think I haven't considered that, eh?" the Kid grated. "Of course he works for The Three! But that's the one reason I wouldn't want him hung! Can't you see that, you fool! If I was thinking of my personal interests tonight, I'd take this man away from all of you. And when I'd finished with him, I'd know everything I want to know, even if I had to turn Apache to find out!"

He recovered himself, releasing Ormond and nodding toward the prisoner. "You're boss here, Whitman," he conceded.

For a moment there was tension singing in the air, for here were purposes and cross-purposes deadlocked, and a man's life hung in the balance. But Tyler Whitman had seen his way.

"He'll hang," Whitman decided, and when he said it he was the Texan again, the man of the whang-leather breed who'd carried his own law along a hundred trails — sometimes cased at his hip, sometimes looped at his saddle-horn. "God knows it won't bring Hanson back to life. But there are other M.P. men who may have to get in the way of bullets in the days to come. Maybe the rest of those wolves will think twice before they line sights on one of my boys!"

The prisoner looked very sick, but he still clung to his poise as though the realization was strong upon him that there was nothing else left to cling to. He dipped his head toward Ormond. "Thanks, mister," he sneered, "for tryin'."

"I didn't try for *your* sake, mister," Ormond snapped. "Get that straight! Hanson was one of my staff, worked under me. You deserve what you're going to get!"

Someone fetched a rope, and grim-faced men who'd worked at the side of yellow-haired Hanson closed in upon the renegade. Somewhere in the shadows Tara drew in her breath, and the sound of it was like a sob. The Kid didn't wait for the rest of the procedure. There was a slump to his shoulders, and a great weariness was upon him as he crossed the trestle to the waiting work train.

9.

In his first day in the service of the Montana-Pacific, the Gospel Kid had had the baptism of fire and fist, conquered a champion and won the respect of the brawny breed who pushed steel toward the setting sun. But at the same time he'd lost the respect of Tara Herndon and openly clashed with Kurt Ormond. The chief engineer, he suspected, would not quickly forgive or forget. And the girl — there was no use denying the truth. He had loved her from the moment of their first meeting. He knew that, now that she had nothing but contempt for him. In the whirl of activity attending the construction of the roaring road, he tried to banish her from his thoughts.

If the days that followed were not so hectic as the first one had been, they were busy days at least, tramping on each other's heels endlessly. April turned into May, with the Kid policing the grading crews and stamping out the last of the dissension among them.

There was excitement too, and danger. The Crowfoot Gulch trestle was repaired without further trouble, but another trestle was blasted skyward. There were nights when the Kid, alert for more sabotage, never saw the cot in the tent that had been assigned to him. But his was the satisfaction of having done his part when the end of steel reached the town of Lazura in record time.

A mile a day, sometimes more, the track had crawled; and the first of June saw the railroad's arrival at Lazura. Thereupon Lazura, scarcely more than a stage-line way station before, took on a new lease of life, for the bubble had burst at Caprock, and the wise ones hurried to this new font of fortune.

Even the Golden Slipper had made the move. True, this was a new Golden Slipper, a flimsy building of wood and canvas designed by Hoyt Durham for transportation from town to town as the railroad pushed westward. But the same bar and mirror and tables were here, freighted overland by Curly Bottsinger. And "The Lady of the Nile" smiled down from a fragile wall upon the thirsty of Lazura town.

Thackery Weaver was there too,

pounding his press in a big tent which now housed his newspaper. The Kid met the editor on Lazura's street shortly afterwards and had to listen to Weaver's enthusiastic babbling.

"It's not the Caprock *Tribune* any more," the owlish-looking little man said. "It's the paper that follows the rails, the *End O' Steel Echo.* When the road is finished, I'll go back to Caprock again."

His voice peevish as another thought struck him, he fixed his weird stare upon the Kid.

"Why didn't you tell me you were Hellvation Hank's brother, that first day in Caprock?" Weaver complained. "Everybody knows it, and everybody has guessed that you're here to avenge Hank. The paper was the last to find it out. I could have given you a mighty nice write-up . . ."

The Kid shouldered on. A score of business places were hanging out the same shingles they had used before, all of them proving the same point. The steel had passed Caprock — therefore Caprock was following the steel.

In a dark alley that first night, the Kid caught a glimpse of a phantom-like figure scurrying along and was sure it was Shadow Loomis. He chased the man, calling his name. He wanted to talk to Loomis, not only because Kurt Ormond had asked him to do so, but to satisfy his own curiosity as well. But Loomis merged with the gloom and was gone. Yet the Kid was certain he'd seen Shadow Loomis, and the thought came to him that only the setting in Lazura was different. The pattern of the puzzle remained the same, and the pieces were all there for the assembling.

A great restlessness was beginning to stir within Matt McGrath. The novelty of the grading camps had worn off for him, and the marching days were bringing him no nearer to his goal.

True, he was seeing the triumph of the Montana-Pacific, for word had come that Central Western's progress was not alarming and that Tyler Whitman's road was definitely ahead in the race to the mountains. That pleased the Kid, for the railroad was the unrealized dream of Hellvation Hank, and the Kid was part of the railroad. But he was no nearer to The Three, and the Kid longed for a change in the routine he was following. Thus Tyler Whitman found him more than responsive when he gave the Kid a special order.

"You'll find the Deadman country yonder," Whitman told him, a wave of his arm indicating the Big Thunders looming above them now, miles away yet seemingly at the end of steel. "There's a beef herd being gathered on that range for delivery to the construction camps. I'd rest easier if you'd meet the herd and make sure it gets here."

"Rustlers?" the Kid asked hopefully.

"Maybe. Or perhaps the herd was never gathered in the first place."

"Don't the Deadman ranchers like the feel of railroad money?"

Whitman frowned. "You might as well know the truth of it," he said. "Storm Herndon of the H-in-a-Hat is king of the Deadman range, and a crusty old codger he is. He hates the railroad and makes no bones about it, figures it will fill the country with sodbusters. Yet in spite of that, Herndon is a friend of mine. We rode range together, along with Hellvation Hank, before we had fuzz on our faces. But if Herndon's got it into his head to buck the road, he'll fight hard. And if he decides to starve us out, the other Deadman ranchers will probably follow his lead. Do you see what you might be up against?"

"Herndon?" the Kid repeated. "Then Tara Herndon, the girl who was on the train into Caprock — ?"

"His daughter," Whitman explained. "Storm had sent her East for schooling, and she was on her way home that night. I had quite a talk with her at the time, and she promised to help us to the extent of seeing that her father fulfilled his original beef contract with M.P. at any rate. I'm sure she'll do it, too."

The Kid let it go at that, asking no more questions. But it was significant that another hour found him in the saddle and upon the plain. He pushed hard that long day until he passed Deadman town, a sleepy, silent huddle of buildings awaiting the magic wand of the Montana-Pacific to awake it from its drowsiness, and he ate supper with the M.P. tunnel crew upon the slope of the Big Thunders when night came. Dawn found him angling northward, skirting the frowning mountain range.

It was wild, rugged country, with up-thrusting ground forming a palisade of cliffs with a stream gurgling at the base of them. Those cliffs were an effective barrier forcing M.P. to swing to the south. The engineering staff had surveyed this country weeks before and decided to detour before drilling a tunnel.

But such matters were beyond the ken of the Kid and held little interest for him.

Circling back upon the prairie again, he scanned the receding horizon carefully. And in the late afternoon he saw what he'd hoped to see, the dust raised by a thousand hoofs as a moving queue of cattle moved stolidly across the range.

The Deadman herd! A half-dozen riders hazed the beef along. There was no chuck-wagon with the outfit, but an open-topped wagon, piled high with supplies, led the cavalcade in the point position, a small figure holding the reins. Putting spurs to his horse, the Kid thundered toward the wagon, whirling his mount to rein short abreast of it.

"Railroad beef?" he asked, and found himself staring into the blue eyes of Tara Herndon.

She made a petite figure in levis and jumper with her flowing curls tucked under a floppy sombrero, and the Kid stared, tongue-tied. In spite of himself, this girl had crowded his thoughts much of the time since their two brief meetings beyond Crowfoot Gulch. There had been hostility in her last glance then, and that same hostility was in her manner now.

"Yes," she said stiffly.

The Kid paced his mount beside her wagon, finding himself very ill at ease.

"Didn't figger I'd find *you* here," he remarked at last.

"This herd belongs to a half-dozen Deadman range spreads. Each outfit has a rep riding with it. I'm here for my dad's H-in-a-Hat."

The Kid grinned. "Storm Herndon's willin' to feed the railroad, eh?"

Tara's chin came up. "He made a bargain with Tyler Whitman last Fall," she said. "He's keeping that bargain. After that he'll decide whether we'll sell more beef to the Montana-Pacific. At first I thought Mr. Whitman was right and Dad was wrong, but now I'm not so sure. What do we want with a railroad on this range?"

"It'll get cattle to market without walkin' the tallow off 'em," the Kid observed. "It'll mean prosperity for the towns along the right o' way."

"Like Caprock?" she mocked. "I came that far in April, remember. Is that your idea of what a town should be like? Drunken men and painted women crowding the streets! After knowing the Caprock we used to have, it sickened me to see it."

He shrugged. "I saw a sawbones operate on a man once," he said. "It was in a hideout down in Texas, and a bunch of us held lanterns to give the medico some light. He didn't have much to work with, and the gent on the table yelled a heap. It shore wasn't pretty, that operation. But afterwards the gent was in better shape than he'd ever been."

She had no answer for that, and he rode in silence beside her. Then, spurred by an impulse, he swung from the saddle to the wagon seat, taking the reins from her hands before she could protest.

"Miss," he said, "I wouldn't mind knowin' what there is about me that makes me look like a sidewinder to you."

Her surprise was genuine. "You don't know why I dislike you?" she asked.

"Not for certain."

She was silent for a long moment. "Hellvation Hank was my friend," she said at last. "He always stopped at the H when he was in the Deadman country. He was a rare man, Hellvation Hank. All he ever owned were the clothes he wore and the leather-bound Bible he carried. Yet he was a whole lot happier than a heap of gents who measured themselves and each other by the acres they owned, the houses they'd built, and the critters they tallied. Can you understand that?"

"Hank was some older than me," said the Kid. "Old enough, you might say, to be my father. So I didn't know him very well. He wrote me right often, but I never saw him after I was a button."

"And you never worried much about him, either," she snapped. "Yet Hellvation Hank loved only two things — his work and his kid brother. Oh, he told me all about you!"

"Must 'a' been a pretty picture," the Gospel Kid observed drily.

"It was as pretty as Hank could make it," Tara retorted. "But he was too honest not to face the truth. Young Matt was down on the border. Matt was running wet cattle across the Rio. Matt was mixed up in some shirt-tail revolution and was smuggling guns into Mexico. Matt's name was linked with a bank robbery in the Panhandle. In fact, it seemed like Matt was in trouble most of the time."

"I'm beginning to savvy," he said slowly. "You know my back-trail pretty well — just as Kurt Ormond knew it, and Ty Whitman, too. That's why I looked like some kind of kill-crazy wolf to you when I wanted to hang that hombre off Crowfoot trestle. You figgered I was too guilty myself to have any right to pass judgment on any other man."

"Does any one have the right to pass

judgment on others?"

He gave that his solemn consideration. Then: "What do you cow folks do with rustlers when you catch 'em on Deadman range?" he wanted to know.

He didn't know that she had a memory of Storm Herndon leaving home with a rifle over his arm, and of silent figures hanging from the cottonwoods afterwards. But her very silence told him he'd scored a point, and he grasped the advantage.

"They hang rustlers in Montana, the same as they do in Texas," he said. "I know. I've rode in the shadow of the rope, myself. When you play a dangerous game, you sorta figure you gotta take the consequences no matter which way the cards fall. That's why that jigger could spit on Ty Whitman's boots and go dangle without battin' an eye. I'd like to think, miss, that if the rope had ever caught up with me in Texas, I could've took my medicine the same way — no matter who was spoonin' it out."

"Maybe hanging that fellow was the only thing that could have been done," she conceded. "But that isn't what I hold against you. Can't you understand what you did to Hank? Don't you see what it meant to him to have a brother who was everything

132

Hank preached against and hated? Don't you see that there couldn't be any real happiness for Hank when he loved you and knew what you were? That's the cross Hellvation Hank carried. And you're the man who loaded it upon his shoulders!"

"But I'm here on account of him," he reminded her.

"Yes," Tara blazed. "To shoot and to kill — to hunt down his murderers and murder in turn! That will be your way, Matt McGrath! I knew it when you spoke your piece to Tyler Whitman that first night!"

"Maybe Hellvation Hank wouldn't mind," he said, remembering things he'd read in his brother's Bible. "Didn't the Israelites have to get a mite rough with the Philistines before they won the Promised Land?"

She had no answer for that either, and the silence that fell between them was broken only by the bawling of the herd and the creak of the wagon. The Kid kept his eyes to the front, and almost a mile of tawny rangeland unreeled before he spoke.

"When a feller is young and headstrong, he forgets a lot of things," he finally remarked. "The mother who kept a lamp in the window for him, for instance, and the father who was stern because his own blood had been hot blood once. And he forgets the brother whose ways weren't his ways. But it's a long trail from Texas, miss, and a man can do a heap of thinking. I preached a funeral service for a girl in a Kansas town. It wasn't my kind of work, but I had a Bible and folks asked me to use it. A heap of people shook my hand afterwards — decent people who wouldn't have looked twice at McGrath of the Rio."

He paused, his voice thick with suffering. "Then I began to savvy why a four-dollar hoss and a saddle held together with haywire was good enough for Hank," he said. "I'd have liked to told Hank about that when I got to Caprock. He's buried there, I hear tell, but I didn't go near the cemetery. You can't talk to a tombstone."

He turned at the pressure of her hand upon his arm and was amazed to see tears jeweling her lashes. "I'm — I'm sorry, Matt," she said. "I guess I didn't understand. And I guess I forgot something I should have remembered, too — something about 'Judge not, lest ye be judged.' Will you forgive me?"

The Gospel Kid smiled, for it was as though a fence had been torn down between them. He'd wanted mightily to

134

restore himself to favor in her eyes, and his heart was singing because he had. After that their talk turned to trivial things as the afternoon waned and dusk stole across the range. Thunderheads were massing about the distant peaks, and heat lightning played above the horizon when they made camp.

Now the Kid had his first chance to meet the trail crew, five salty riders from as many different spreads. There was bow-legged Banty Ryan of the Moonbar; and the Denny twins, Freckles and Chick, who rode for the adjoining Rafter B and Circle 7 spreads — two youngsters scarcely out of their teens. Dave Woods represented the Flying V, and lanky Ike Tonkin was there for his own Tumbled T. The Kid liked them all instinctively, but he wrung hands rather hurriedly, for his interest was centered in the signs of a coming storm, and his concern was for the bedded herd.

"Looks like hell's a-gonna be cuttin' loose," old Banty Ryan reflected from the depth of his experience, and thereby voiced the Kid's own thought.

"After chuck, I'll take the first watch," the Kid volunteered.

In the saddle again, he rode across the flats toward the herd, a darker bulk against the crowding darkness. Circling the bedded beasts, he sang softly to them, humming the same toneless tune that had been upon his lips when he'd ridden toward Crowfoot Gulch weeks before. A few drops of rain spattered against him, and the sky growled a deep-voiced threat.

Yet the Kid knew a measure of contentment at that moment; a certain nostalgia held him. Born to the saddle, he was doing his own kind of work once again. And he was remembering the half-forgotten dream of every wandering cowpoke — the dream of a spread of his own and a herd to bear his brand. But at the same time, the Kid was also uneasy, for the feeling was strong upon him that the darkness cloaked unseen forces; forces which were no less potent because they weren't visible.

There was a nameless *something* out there in the night, a something the Kid could feel without being able to define it. And that part of his mood might have been contagious, for the cattle showed signs of restlessness, snorting irritably while horns rattled.

Minutes lengthened into an hour, and deep darkness swathed the land as the Kid continued to ride circle. A winking eye of fire had marked the distant camp where the weary riders slumbered, but now the fire had died away. The Kid's uneasiness grew, becoming a clamoring presentiment of danger. And then it happened.

First, rifles banged in the distance, barking yonderly where the camp lay. Then suddenly the night was alive with riders, men who materialized out of the gloom with thundering guns. They swept down upon the far side of the herd, those raiders of the night, shouting and blazing away as they came. It was like touching fire to a split-second fuse. Scared snorts became wild bellows as the cattle, already spooked, exploded into action. Then the herd was surging across the range in mad stampede. And in the midst of it, a chip tossed on that torrent of fear-crazed beef, the Kid was swept along. No longer did Gospel thoughts hold him. He was the Stampede Kid now!

Ride the stampede! That was all Matt could do. His long body flattened out over his mount's neck, he was carried forward by the fury of the herd's wild rush. It was dangerous enough to be swept along by the maddened steers; it would be certain death to try and check the crazed creatures. Yet in the midst of peril, the Kid's real fear was not for himself but for Tara. Guns still popped in the distance, which meant the raiders were keeping the camp busy.

Who were these horsemen of the night? Henchmen of The Three — hirelings of Central Western — independent rustlers who'd sighted prime beef, theirs for the taking? It didn't matter just now. Whoever they were, they'd struck — and struck hard.

With Tara's peril to goad him, the Kid began a desperate play. Reining carefully, he forced his horse toward the fringe of the herd. It was slow, nerve-racking work, for a single misstep might send horse and rider down beneath those thundering hoofs.

Yonderly and ahead was a bit of higher ground, dim in the darkness, and the Kid inched toward it. If he could gain that slight promontory, the herd might split and go around him. But the bluff seemed a million miles away, and steers were still bolting past him as he angled toward it. Thirty feet — twenty — ten — In a few seconds he'd be forcing his horse up the bluff, climbing to safety. But that was when disaster overtook him.

The Kid was never to know exactly how it happened. Perhaps a gopher hole tripped his mount — perhaps the horse lost its footing trying to dodge the raking, razor-edged horn of a fear-crazed steer. Whatever the cause, the horse suddenly stumbled, and the Kid, caught off balance, sailed over its head. He tried frantically to twist himself so he might land on all fours. But the ground was rushing upward, a blinding light exploded before his eyes, and a greater darkness engulfed him . . .

10.

After the Gospel Kid had ridden out to the bedded herd, Tara Herndon, busy with after-chuck chores at the wrecking pan, found herself thinking of him. Humming as she worked, the girl freely admitted to herself that the lean young Texan interested her greatly, had from the first. She was remembering many things about him, but mostly she remembered their talk of the afternoon when Matt McGrath had revealed a side to his nature which she hadn't known existed.

Ruthless and deadly, he'd seemed at first, a man with a driving will that would brook no interference with the undertaking that had brought him to Montana. But today he'd shown another face, spoken of his new-found respect for his brother. This new Matt McGrath, Tara decided, was very much to her liking.

The weary trail crew was soon ready to bed down. Tara had had all the help she needed with her chores. There were almost as many men snatching at floursack dish-towels as there were dishes to be dried; old

Banty Ryan and lanky Ike Tonkin being as eager as the younger cowpokes to lend a hand. After that boots and belts were peeled off as each sought his own blankets, and Tara bedded among them, chaperoned by the very nature of these men.

There'd been a few drops of rain already. Tara, her face to the sullen sky, heard the repeated mutter of thunder, and her mind turned again to the man who kept a lonely vigil yonderly where the herd was held. But none of the restlessness that the Kid was feeling at that moment was conveyed to her. Instead she felt a deep serenity, a feeling of peace which she could neither define nor analyze but which she knew, somehow, was related to the new understanding between herself and Matt McGrath.

In the midst of it, hell broke loose.

Thunder exploded now, for sure, but it wasn't the sky that was speaking with fiery tongues, and the rain that lashed the camp was a leaden rain, pouring from the darkness. It brought all five cowmen out of their blankets. Tara was on her feet at the same time, frantically pulling on her boots and strapping a gunbelt about her middle as her sleepy companions barked questions at each other.

"Rustlers!" Ike Tonkin shouted in

sudden understanding. At the same time the Tumbled T man thumbed his gun, scattering lead to answer the lethal challenge from out yonder.

Banty Ryan and Dave Woods and the Denny twins had grasped the situation by now. "Down!" Freckles Denny roared, and forced Tara to the ground, throwing himself prone at the same time. The others followed suit, spreading out and returning the withering fire as fast as they could shoot. The wagon offered some shelter, and Dave Woods rolled under it, dragging Tara after him.

"Who are they?" the girl wanted to know. She was using her own gun as effectively as any of the men. But there was nothing to shoot at but gunflashes, elusive targets at best. Whoever was out there was mounted, a group of horsemen circling the camp Indian-fashion, firing as they rode.

"Hard sayin' who those jaspers are," Dave Woods jerked out. "You've been East for a spell, so maybe you don't know about all the rustlin' that's been goin' on. A bunch of longriders has been workin' all the way from here to the Caprock country. They always strike during a storm, too. A pretty foxy bunch."

Tara punched fresh cartridges into her

gun. "They picked a good night," she reflected gloomily.

"And McGrath's out there alone with the herd," Woods groaned. "What chance has he got?"

A certain doubt speared through Tara then. This raid of the rustlers coincided with the appearance of Matt McGrath — McGrath of the Rio whose reputation along the brimstone border hadn't been any too savory. She wouldn't have been human if she hadn't felt suspicion's thrust, for she was remembering, among other things, that he'd volunteered to do the night-hawking.

But no, this was railroad beef, a herd consigned to Tyler Whitman. If the Gospel Kid had proved nothing else by his actions, he'd at least proved his loyalty to the Montana-Pacific. And with that thought, the last doubt vanished and she felt thoroughly ashamed because the doubt had existed, even for a moment.

"It'll be bad for him," she said, tight-lipped. "It's the cattle they're after. They're keeping us busy here while they run off the herd. Listen — !" Above the roar of gunfire and the sibilant hiss of the rain, which was falling with a vengeance now, came the rumble of thundering hoofs, ominous and unmistakable. "They've stamped it already! Matt — !"

"We'll be able to give him a hand," Woods assured her. "Them gents ain't tryin' to do any damage to us. They're just shooting enough to keep us ground-anchored here. But once we get out of this, we'll —"

He clutched at his throat, blood oozing between his fingers as his words dissolved into a meaningless mutter. It took a full second for Tara to realize he'd been hit, another before she knew that this thing slumping against her was still warm with life, though there was no life in it.

"Dave!" she cried. "Dave!" Her voice rose, shrill with grief and anger. "They got Dave, boys!" she sobbed. "He's dead!"

It was as though she had ordered a charge. Her announcement was like a whip, lashing the crew into desperation, prodding them out to where death waited. No word passed between them, but suddenly Ike Tonkin and Banty Ryan and the Denny twins were jackknifing erect, charging into the darkness. And at their heels, her fury no less than theirs, came Tara.

A rope corral held the cavvy, a rearing, plunging bunch of horses. Saddles were slapped on recklessly, cinches tightened hurriedly. Then the five were mounted, fanning wide into the night. But Tara, sawing at the reins, stared about her into the sleazy blackness and realized that the enemy was gone. There was no one to fight.

The herd was gone too, vanished into the darkness to the west. With the herd would be the raiders. They'd besieged the camp until their coup was accomplished. Then the night had swallowed them, and the rain had drawn a curtain after them. It was an angry and disgruntled group that gathered to consider the situation.

"It's easy to figger why those gents always choose a stormy night to strike," old Banty Ryan observed. "This rain'll blot out sign pronto. We gotta take the trail while there is a trail. Let's be ridin'."

There was no word spoken about Dave Woods who was lying under the wagon, staring with sightless eyes. They'd bury him later. That was understood. And that was how Dave Woods, who'd drawn thirty a month and chow from the Flying V, would want it. And there was no mention made of Matt McGrath, who might be lying dead upon the prairie, leveled by rustler lead or trampled beneath the stampede. Cattle came first, by cattleland's creed. A dead man needed no help, and a living man could take care of himself.

Yet Tara tried to study the dark terrain as they rode along, and it wasn't always the spoor of the vanishing herd she was seeking. Yonderly was a bluff, grotesque blotch of darkness against the darkness — the bluff the Kid had spied. But the Deadman crew gave it a wide berth. If rustlers had lingered behind to prevent pursuit, the concealment of the bluff would afford a good place for ambush.

The rain was really beating down now, increasing in its fury, and occasional lightning flashes illuminated the land. In the chalky glare Tara saw the faces of her companions, stern and bleak, their eyes always to the front. Then darkness would come to blot out the scene as they pushed onward.

And so the slow hours paced, with the trail wending ever westward until cliffs reared ahead, the same cliffs the Kid had skirted when he'd come to meet the herd. The crew held another consultation then, risking a cupped match to cut sign. It didn't make sense that the herd would still be pushed in that direction, with the barrier ahead. But there was no deviation from the original course.

"Something's loco here," Ike Tonkin muttered. "But if they want to ride smack into the river that runs along the bottom of the cliffs, I reckon we're just the huckleberries to follow 'em."

He'd voiced the mystification of all of them and the determination as well. They pushed on in silence, alert now for anything to happen. But when they neared the stream that paralleled the base of the cliffs, a lightning flash gave them a view they hadn't expected to see.

They were much closer to the stolen herd than they'd supposed. The cattle, spent and weary after their wild stampede, had set their own slow pace, and they had almost overtaken them. But that wasn't the thing that stiffened Tara in her saddle. The cattle were being shoved into the stream, hazed straight across it toward the rocky wall that towered upward! It didn't make sense — but it was so. Shapeless in the night, riders flanked the herd, urging it on. At least one rustler was in drag position. That much Tara saw while the lightning endured.

Banty Ryan shoved back his floppy sombrero and raked his expanse of baldness with stubby fingers. "I don't savvy it," he admitted freely. "If they was rustlin' fish or frawgs, it might make sense. But it looks like a chance to even up for pore Dave and maybe spread a little confusion among those sinners. Keepin' them critters from swimmin' downstream is gonna keep them galoots plumb busy crossin' that crick. If we charged 'em now —"

"Wait!" Tara gasped, for the lightning was forking across the heavens again. And if they'd been amazed to see the cattle shoved into the stream, they were doubly astounded to see the ultimate destination of the herd.

A narrow shelf at the cliff's base formed the farther bank of the stream — a brush-cluttered bank, not many feet wide. But the land was weirdly lighted for a moment, and that bank was revealed suddenly barren of bushes. Where the bushes had been was a gaping hole, probably eight feet high, an inky-black opening against the whiteness of the cliffs. Into that opening the steers were being forced, one at a time.

"*A tunnel!*" Freckles Denny shrilled. "Jumpin' Jehosophat — a tunnel right back into the cliff!"

His twin echoed his astonishment, but the others, the older men and Tara, were silent before the portent of this. For amazing as this discovery was, the significance of it was even more amazing. It was like having a mystery of the ages explained away in a few brief words. It was like reading a page that had always been blank. No mystery now as to why these raiders always struck on a stormy night when the rain would obliterate sign. No secret why beef seemingly vanished from the face of the earth.

"A tunnel," Ike Tonkin said at last. "No wonder we used to figger we was chasin' shadows when we took the trail of rustled beef. Boys, I'm thinkin' we've done a mighty good night's work."

"Let's be gettin' on," Banty Ryan said eagerly. "I crave to see what's at the other end o' that tunnel."

Undoubtedly the wisest thing would have been to have gone for re-enforcements, gathered enough cattlemen to meet any menace that might lie ahead. They were only five, and they had no means of gauging the strength of the rustler force. And they had gained enough by stumbling upon the secret of their hideout.

But there wasn't a man among the crew who would have turned back now if the devil's own legion had waited beyond. Curiosity can be more potent than the threat of peril, and adventure has a lure that doesn't count the costs. Even Tara felt the pull of it, and her ears were deaf to Banty Ryan's covert suggestion.

"Now if you was to wait here, miss, until we come back —" he began. "It could be a mite risky yonder, and if you was to —"

Her chin came up. "Some of those critters yonder are wearing a H-in-a-Hat burned on them," she reminded him. "I'll trail along."

If experience had taught these men that you didn't cross old Storm Herndon, intuition must have told them that arguing with his daughter would be just as useless.

"You be keerful, miss," Banty compromised lamely, and then the quintet was pushing forward again. Forcing their reluctant horses into the stream, they found it to be little more than stirrup-deep, and they soon splashed across it and onto the ledge. The bushes had been put back into place, they discovered, the shrubbery that camouflaged the entrance. Dismounting, they carefully picked their way among them and into the hidden tunnel.

"A nacheral tunnel!" Banty marveled in a whisper, and the echo amplified his remark to alarming proportions. After that they all kept silence, leading their horses in single file, for the tunnel was wide enough in some places but allowed no more than the passage of a single mount at a time in other places. They didn't risk a light, groping along an inch at a time. But the tunnel ran straight ahead, and it was less than half a mile long. They emerged into deep darkness and huddled together instinctively.

"Could use that lightning now," Chick Denny squeaked in a voice that didn't sound like his own.

The rain was beginning to abate, but his wish was answered by a sudden flare across the sky. Then they were treated to the greatest surprise in this night of surprises, for a valley lay before them, a valley hidden away here behind the cliffs, a valley as primitive and as pretty as Eden must have been. They had a brief glimpse of cabins and corrals not far away.

"A perfect hideout," Tara breathed. "Any other entrance to this valley must be back in the Big Thunders and almost inaccessible. It might have been a thousand years before any one stumbled upon this place. I —"

Somewhere in the murky darkness a boot heel crunched against stone, the sound freezing her words in her throat. The lightning had showed her that all her companions were close beside her. Tara stiffened to a premonition of danger, her darting fingers instinctively closing upon the butt of her six-gun.

"Who's there?" she challenged.

At first there was only silence, but the very silence was pregnant with some nameless danger. Then the darkness became alive, for men were threshing among the bushes that screened this inner entrance to the tunnel. It was like being beset by shadows, for there was nothing to be seen. And yet the menace was there, surrounding them in the darkness, closing in upon them relentlessly. Raising her gun, Tara fired once. Then a rough hand was closing upon her wrist, wrenching the gun away from her.

"Stand hitched — all of you!" a voice rasped, almost in Tara's ear, and the lightning flared again. In its chalky glare she saw them, the raiders they'd been trailing, eight men ringing the Deadman crew with leveled guns.

"We figgered you was pretty close behind us," one of the raiders said. "You hankered to see what was at the tunnel's end, eh? Just plumb curious! And now you know!"

Despair choked Tara — despair and fear. They had stumbled upon a secret that would spell the finish of all these rustlers, once it was revealed. Dangerous knowledge! And worthless knowledge, for their curiosity had been greater than their caution, leading them into a trap from which there might be no escaping.

11.

The lash of rain against his face brought the Gospel Kid back to consciousness. Opening his eyes, he vaguely realized that he was sprawled upon sloping ground. He'd reached the bluff after all. His vision was clear enough, but his head ached, and his mind remained shrouded in fog. At first his whereabouts had no significance for him, and he lay there trying to coordinate his thoughts. There'd been guns, he remembered, and a stampede, and —

Tara — ! The herd — ! With the rush of memory, he sat up to find himself quite alone. Only the sibilant sound of the rain broke the silence, and the first flash of lightning revealed an endless vista of prairie, naked of any living thing except his horse. The bay stood nearby, reins trailing, regarding him patiently.

Apparently the mount hadn't been crippled by its fall; and if it had bolted, it had also returned. Painfully the Kid pulled himself into the saddle and rode toward the distant campsite. He started uneasily when he found it to be a silent, deserted place. The wagon still stood there, and Dave Woods sprawled beneath it, his sightless eyes staring into the sloppy heavens, a bullet hole in his throat. It wasn't the rain that chilled the Kid then. Tara was gone, and so were the others — Banty Ryan, Ike Tonkin, and the Denny twins.

Prisoners? It didn't make sense that the raiders would take prisoners. But the Deadman crew certainly wasn't there, so the Kid headed west. The herd had been stampeded in that direction, and somewhere to the west he might find those he sought. It was as good a theory as any, and his mood demanded action of some sort.

Trailing wasn't easy, for the rain had increased in fury. But the sign was plain enough in the sodden ground, although it would be washed away by morning if the storm continued. By cupping matches from time to time, the Kid managed to assure himself that he was on the right trail. He had no way of knowing how long he'd lain unconscious, but he soon came to realize that it couldn't have been long. The trail was fresh enough to prove there hadn't been any great lapse of time. But most of the night was gone before the chalky glare of a lightning flash gave him a glimpse of the herd far ahead.

He was overtaking it! Riders were hazing the spent cattle along, but there was no way of identifying them at such a distance, especially since the light lasted for only a second, and then deeper darkness descended. The fact that the herd was still being headed *away* from camp proved that those riders were the rustlers, and not the Deadman crew. The Kid's impulse was to put spurs to his horse, but he restrained himself. Caution might be his most potent weapon now.

He was beginning to recognize this country, which was some slight advantage. He was nearing those palisading cliffs he had skirted the day before. They reared themselves straight ahead, due west, which meant — to the Kid's way of thinking — that the herd would have to angle, either to the north or the south.

He was out of the saddle and tightening a cinch when the next flash came, the same flash that gave Tara and her companions their glimpse of the herd being forced into the stream at the base of the cliffs. Thus he did not see that spectacle. He'd had a glimpse of a group of shadowy riders a ways behind the herd, and his heart had leaped with the thought that it might be the Deadman crew, hot on the trail. But there was also a chance that it might be a rear-guard of rustlers. He'd find out in due time, the Kid promised himself.

The shallow stream was whipped to a semblance of fury by the rain when the Kid stood upon its bank not long after. Risking a match, he saw sign plainly enough. The herd had been forced into the stream. The Kid, schooled along shadowy trails, smiled at such an ancient ruse.

The storm would erase sign, but the raiders were taking no chances, the Kid guessed. Let a wrathful posse of Deadman ranchers come riding in search of their vanished herd. Let them find sign, if any existed, for the sign would dead-end on the banks of the stream. Somewhere to the north or south the cattle would come to solid footing again.

That was the way the Kid had it figured, and it was pat enough. He was satisfied with his own reasoning — and annoyed too. Now he could trail only by guesswork, and there were two directions to take. He might have chosen one of them and headed either north or south, had not a sound reached him, so faint as to be a mere shadow of a sound. Yet he recognized it for what it was. A shot! And the Kid could have sworn it had been fired directly across the stream!

His eyes strained, the Kid waited impatiently for the next lightning flash. The rain was beginning to abate, but the lightning came again, giving him a glimpse of the narrow strip of shore on the farther side. There was certainly no place to hide a herd of cattle on that skimpy shelf, clogged with willows and bushes and with the cliffs rearing upward behind them.

But that shot had come from across the stream, he reminded himself emphatically. Forcing his reluctant horse into the stream and finding the water no more than belly-deep to the animal, he prodded the bay to the other shore.

And there, threshing among the dripping bushes on that narrow strip of land, he made another discovery — one that stiffened him in his saddle with surprise. Those bushes had no roots! They were piled there in such a manner as to appear natural to a casual eye on the distant bank. But they were camouflage, screening the mouth of a tunnel leading back under the cliff.

The Kid whistled low and tonelessly as he made that discovery. A tunnel — a cleverly-concealed tunnel! No wonder the herd had vanished! Probably a hundred other herds had vanished from the Deadman country in like fashion. With a storm to wash out sign, the raiders had the means of making cattle seemingly disappear from the face of the earth! A stranger to the Deadman range, the Kid was no stranger to the possibilities this thing held.

Out of his saddle, he cautiously edged into the tunnel, leading his horse after him. The silence of a tomb brooded there. As the Kid stole forward, he risked a match or two on the way. This was a natural tunnel, he discovered, formed, perhaps, by some subterranean river that had ran there once, only to have its course changed by some upheaval of nature in ages past. The floor was dry and rocky underfoot, and the ceiling curved above, never less than ten feet high, sometimes twice that height.

The tunnel was straight as an arrow, with a faint glow of light marking its farther end. When the Kid emerged, he found a rain-washed moon fighting to pierce the storm-scudded sky, and in that feeble light he passed a hand before his unbelieving eyes. Before him spread a valley, a lush valley curving westwardly. And not half a mile away sprawled two cabins and a mammoth peeled-pole corral that held the snorting herd intended for the Montana-Pacific.

Here was a perfect hideout. The Kid was quick to recognize its perfection. Rustlers could hold beef there forever, if necessary, leisurely blotting brands before hazing them on to some dubious markets. Meanwhile, irate cattlemen could scour the range beyond the cliffs in vain.

But the Kid wasn't interested in cattle at that moment, nor in the possibilities this place afforded to those who knew its secret entrance. Where were Tara and her friends? Were they prisoners here? One of the cabins was dark and silent, but the other, the nearer one, huddled in the shadow of a cutbank that towered beside it, had light flowing from its windows. Tying his horse in a clump of dripping bushes, the Kid eased toward the nearest window and raised his eyes above the sill.

Eight men were inside. The Kid could count them in the glow of a flickering lamp set upon a split-log table which shared honors with a pot-bellied stove, some built-in bunks and a few chairs as the only furnishings of the place. Eight men . . . There were big men and little men, and one of them was obviously Mexican, and their only resemblance to each other was a

160

common stamp of viciousness all of them wore.

They were talking among themselves as they discarded dripping garments. One of them knelt to shave kindling for a fire. The Kid didn't tarry to try to hear what they were saying. These were the raiders, without a doubt. The Kid was interested in prisoners. Therefore he crept toward the other cabin.

The second cabin had only one window, a small affair, entirely too small to allow the passage of a human body. But there were humans inside, the Kid knew at once, for he heard their restless movements and the faint murmur of their voices. Scratching on the window sill, he ventured a whispered, "Tara . . . ?"

A moment later the window swung inward. "Matt?" the girl whispered excitedly.

"You all right?" he asked. "And the boys? They in there?"

"All except Dave Woods of the Flying V. He was killed when the camp was attacked. And Chick Denny has just admitted that he was nicked, but he isn't badly hurt. Are you all right, Matt?"

He told her what had happened to him. Then: "What sort of game are those snaky gents playin'?" he wanted to know. "Why did they fetch you here?"

"They didn't, really," the girl explained. "We trailed the raiders until they reached the creek, and we thought it was a good place to rush them. But they were too cagy for us. They prodded the beef into that amazing tunnel and ambushed us as we trailed after them. And we walked right into their trap! I managed to fire just once before they took my gun away from me."

"I heard the shot," the Kid said. "A lucky thing I did, too. You must have been standing almost in the mouth of the tunnel or the sound would never have carried through the cliffs."

Anger stirred him as a new thought crossed his mind. "You shouldn't have taken the trail, girl. The boys shouldn't have let you!"

"They didn't want to, Matt. But I'm representing the H, remember!"

The Kid shrugged, seeing no point in arguing a matter when argument couldn't change the situation any. He slipped to the door of the cabin, found it fastened by a heavy padlock, and came back to report his discovery.

"I could blast it off with my gun," he said. "But the bunch in yonder cabin would hear the shot and be on our necks pronto, long before we'd have time to find horses and get onto 'em. Nope, it would be too risky to try that. Any idea what they figger on doing with your outfit?"

"Hard sayin'," Ike Tonkin spoke up. "It looks mighty bad, though. They never intended for us to learn the secret of this hideout. They can't let us lope off with that under our hats!"

"It's beginning to get light," the Kid observed. "I'm duckin' for cover before they find me here. But don't be worryin'. I'll be close by, waitin' my chance. Once they leave you alone for a spell, I'll have that door open mighty fast."

He gave Tara his hand through the window, and she gripped it hard, the four cowpokes crowding behind her to whisper brief words of caution and advice. Then the Kid was blending with the shadows. Circling the other cabin warily, he climbed to the lip of the cutbank overlooking it. Stretching himself prone, he waited, shaping and discarding a dozen plans.

It was a ticklish situation any way he sized it up. Tara and the Deadman riders had stumbled upon a secret which must have been jealously guarded by rustlers down through the years. Only a grave could hold such a secret inviolate. Yet even these hardened hombres would surely hesitate to murder a woman in cold blood.

Such was the Kid's only consoling thought. But when the eight rustlers trooped out of the cabin in the first pale flush of dawn to stand ringed below him, the Kid, studying those beard-stubbled faces, had to admit that most of them looked capable of anything.

And it was then he decided to make his play. They were directly beneath him, and the cutbank was no more than twelve feet high. He could throw a gun on them from there, hold them at bay and force them to fork over the key to the padlocked cabin. It would be risky work — risky because the odds were eight-to-one. There was a strong chance that at least one of them would go for a gun, thus forcing a powder-smoke play. If that happened, he'd down some of them. But he'd go down himself against such superior odds.

However, that risk would have to be taken, the Kid grimly decided. If he waited, they might leave the vicinity long enough to give him time to get the prison-cabin open. But on the other hand, they might not.

Very cautiously he reached to ease his

gun out of leather. That slight movement was his undoing. He'd forgotten how close he was to the lip of the cutbank. And he'd forgotten that the rain of the night before might have weakened his precarious perch. The earth gave away with a sound like the crack of a gun. Clawing at the air, the Kid found himself tumbling downward in a shower of dirt and gravel, sprawling into the midst of those eight men below.

12.

A half-dozen guns cleared holsters before the Kid lighted, and he sat up to find himself facing them and staring into a ring of scowling faces. At least he'd landed without injuring himself, the Kid reflected, but found scant consolation in the thought. He'd have preferred to have fallen on top of at least one of these eight and rendered him *hors de combat,* thus lessening the odds. For now the Kid was truly in a tight — and nobody knew it better than he.

This certainly wasn't the way he'd intended to announce his presence to these raiders! His mind was racing desperately as he sat up. It was bluff or die! The Kid recognized that fact instantly, so he chose a wry grin for his weapon and managed to force it across his face.

"Now some gents hallo a camp before they come into it," he observed cheerfully. "Me, I've got my own way of making noise. Howdy, boys."

"Just who the hell are you, mister?" snarled the biggest of the eight, a broad-faced, bearded giant, almost as immense as Curly Bottsinger. "And how did you get here?"

The very fact that the fellow bothered to ask such questions gave the Kid his first hope. He'd expected to be greeted by gunfire, not by questions. But if they were willing to postpone his death, even for a minute, the Kid was certainly willing to accept the reprieve.

"South is my name," said the Kid. "Dusty South. I caught a glimpse of you gents pushing yon beef herd through the storm last night. Damned if you didn't haze it right through a wall — a rock wall. 'Dusty,' I sez, 'either you're loco or full of forty-rod busthead. It just ain't natural for cow critters to walk through a wall.' I got so plumb curious that I trailed along."

"A curious gent, eh?" the big man growled ominously. "I'm thinkin' —"

A lean, snaky man whose face seemed to be mostly nose sidled up to the big leader. "He's one of 'em, Cisco," he said emphatically. "He's a Deadman waddy we didn't bag last night. What are you wastin' time on him for?"

"I ain't so sure," big Cisco argued. "I studied the crew through glasses yesterday morning, remember. There was five cowpokes and the gal drivin' the wagon. You boys was plumb sure you got one of them cowpokes when we salivated the camp last night. Another of 'em was holdin' the herd, but he must 'a' got away and joined the others after the raid. We got four of 'em and the gal here, ain't we? That makes this jigger a stray."

He pinned a quick glance on the Kid. "Where's your hoss?"

The Kid jerked his thumb. "Yonder in the bushes," he admitted, without a trace of hesitation.

"Take a look-see at its brand, Shark," Cisco ordered, and the big-nosed man hurried to obey. He was back quickly enough.

"A bay with a brand I never saw before, Yawberry," he reported reluctantly. "It ain't from the Deadman range. And the gear is shore enough Texas."

"Texas!" Cisco Yawberry repeated, and eyed the Kid again. "Just what was it fetched you from Texas, mister?" he demanded.

The Kid grinned again. "Maybe I was drove instead of fetched," he said. "Now I ain't askin' you no questions, am I? Can't a gent keep his back-trail to himself? I don't see no badges pinned on you boys!"

168

It was like teetering on the edge of a volcano, this word-sparring. The Kid wondered how long it would last. But he was still alive, a miracle in itself, for these hombres had the look of men who might have killed him first and asked questions afterwards. There was young Dave Woods to be remembered.

It was the very boldness of his attitude that was his salvation, the Kid guessed. He'd aroused their curiosity and their grudging admiration as well, perhaps. And because boldness had served him well so far, the Kid pursued his brash policy with an assurance he was far from feeling.

"Do I smell coffee boiling in yonder *cabana?*" he asked easily. "Me, I'd shore like some. It's one cure for what a wet night can do to an hombre."

He was studying the rustlers all the while. He'd seen a thousand faces along Montana-Pacific's right of way, had the Kid, and he couldn't know whether or not he'd seen these eight before. What was more significant — he couldn't be sure whether they'd ever seen him. But the Kid had been at end of steel most of this last month, and he was certain this crew hadn't been among the workers — so sure that he was gambling on that point. And he was

169

winning, for it was obvious that they hadn't recognized him, in any case.

Cisco Yawberry slowly pouched his gun. "Fetch him a cup of coffee," the rustler ordered.

Squatting cross-legged, the Kid took the steaming cup when it was handed to him. One by one, the eight dropped to the ground, forming a semi-circle facing him as he sipped the muddy coffee. Following Yawberry's cue, all the rustlers had leathered their irons. But they were eyeing the Kid warily; especially the snaky, big-nosed man who answered to the name of Shark Lund.

The Kid might have been one of them at that moment, yet he knew how fragile was this spell he'd cast by his apparent fearlessness.

By his own admission, he'd trailed them there. What was more to the point, he possessed dangerous knowledge — the secret of the tunnel which served them so well. That made him just as much a menace to their security as those five prisoners who also knew of this hideout. Chances were, his fate would be the same as theirs.

That was why the Kid decided on the most desperate bluff of all — a bluff which would shorten his life to the span of a second if it were called. He didn't dwell on that thought. Instead he cursed and reached for his gun, speaking rapidly as he made the move. The outcome of this play was going to depend on how fast he could talk, rather than on how fast he could unlimber his gun.

"You're not collecting Montana-Pacific head money on me!" he snarled. *"I ain't bein' taken alive, savvy!"*

He'd moved so quickly as to catch them unawares. But though he'd wrenched his gun from leather, he might have died then. There were eight of them, and if they'd responded by going for their own guns, at least one of them would have gotten him. But they stared open-mouthed instead.

"Montana-Pacific head money!" Cisco Yawberry echoed, his massive jaw dropping. "You sayin' the railroad's got a price on you?"

"Don't stall!" the Kid spat. "You know damn well it has! You're figgerin' on packin' my pelt to Tyler Whitman. I could see it in the eyes of every damn one of you while you was watchin' me!"

"Why is Whitman hankerin' for your scalp?" Cisco Yawberry demanded.

"You're bluffin'," the Kid laughed jeeringly. "You've heard about it. You know

I'm the gent who put a bullet through that long-geared Texas trouble-shooter of M.P.'s in Lazura the other day."

"*McGrath!* Us boys has heard tell o' him. You killed that gent?"

"As dead as he's ever goin' to be!" the Kid snarled. "I knew him in Texas, savvy. I promised him there'd be smoke the next time our trails crossed."

Yawberry grinned broadly. "Put away yore gun, Dusty," he advised. "You got us plumb wrong. See that herd corralled yonder? That's beef Montana-Pacific graders figgered they was gonna eat. Does that sound like we're friendly-like with Tyler Whitman?"

His ruse had worked! That was the Kid's triumphant thought, but in the midst of it he knew an overpowering temptation. He had this crew under his gun. Why not force the play through in the way he'd planned before the cutbank had caved? Why not make them release the prisoners?

But no. He'd been willing to take the risk before, but the Kid thought differently now. He'd convinced them that he was a wanted man. There was such a thing as pushing luck too far. Besides, he'd just paved the way for a better opportunity. For Tara's sake, he had to play this game the safest way.

"Rustlers, eh?" the Kid said, and grinned as he pouched his gun. "Now that's what I sorta figgered at first, and I tagged along last night in the hopes that you could use another hand. But the way you gents kept lookin' at me, I wasn't sure how you stood."

"You're among friends," Yawberry assured him. "Any gent that's had the snake sign put on him by Montana-Pacific can ride with this outfit."

"Just a minute, Cisco," Shark Lund put in. "I ain't so sure about this jigger. It's for the boss to say whether he's O.K. or not, savvy!"

Cisco Yawberry bristled belligerently. "Wa-al, he's stayin' here until the boss shows up — which should be tonight or tomorrow sometime. The boss can decide what we'll do with them Deadman cow-pokes and the gal, and he can likewise size up Dusty. And I'm thinkin' he'll sign up this salty gent right pronto."

For a moment the eyes of Yawberry and Lund clashed, but the Kid, watching them, said nothing. He hadn't hoped to win them all over. But at least Yawberry, who appeared to be first in command here, had accepted him.

Nevertheless the Kid was tense with the

knowledge that the real chief of this outfit would be along shortly. When that man came, the doom of the prisoners would undoubtedly be sealed speedily enough. Meantime, though, there might be the sort of opportunity the Kid was playing for. And in any case, he still had his gun . . .

Such was the beginning of the longest day in the Kid's life. He spent the greater part of it squatting in the shadow of the cabin, moving only as the sun moved, shaping cigarettes endlessly in the shade and spinning windies along with the rest of them.

The Gospel Kid had a part to play — and he played it well. He might have been as ruthless as any of them, according to his yarns, and he impressed some of them at least. Shark Lund watched him covertly, but the Kid paid the big-nosed man no heed. He'd gathered that Lund was jealous of Yawberry's position as head man of this bunch, and it was the Kid's guess that Lund would automatically dislike anyone who appeared to stand in favor with Yawberry. But even Lund was less frigid in his attitude toward the Kid before noon came.

With the sun standing high, a pock-marked little man whose swarthy skin betrayed his mixed blood cooked a meal. Afterwards the man took a portion of the unsavory food to the other cabin. The Kid watched indolently as the fellow fished a key from his pocket, unpadlocked the door and, with a gun in his free hand, slid the food inside. The door was immediately locked again.

It was the Kid's hope that something would take the rustler crew away from the cabins during the afternoon. If they left, he'd have to go with them, he knew, but he might be able to slip away from them long enough to return and release the prisoners. Certainly there wasn't a chance with them loitering about the cabin. But as the hours dragged on, the eight still loafed about, patently intending to do nothing. The corralled cattle weren't even turned loose to graze, or taken to water, and their irritable bawling became a nerve-racking thing.

Some of the rustlers mended bridles, hunkering near a pile of gear stacked beside a makeshift corral behind the cabins, a small corral which held the horses of the prisoners and their captors. One rustler whittled lazily while two others stretched themselves upon the ground, their sombreros tilted over their noses, and snatched some sleep during the heat of the day.

Watching them, the Kid sighed. Then, convinced that no opportunity would present itself to help the prisoners while there was daylight, the Kid also took a nap. He was weary and might need renewed strength before another sun-up.

Thus the endless day passed and dusk came at long last to purple the hidden valley as the sun vanished into the maw of the Big Thunders. Felipe, the cook, stirred himself to activity, but only after being urged profanely by his fellows. It was dark before supper was eaten. Afterwards Felipe again headed for the other cabin.

Now the Kid came to his feet, yawning and stretching himself, an indolent act which gave no hint of the excitement throbbing within him. The time had come to force a play, he'd decided. He'd waited for an opportunity and none had come — so now he'd make his own opportunity.

Someone had lighted a lamp in the cabin. Already a poker game was claiming the attention of most of the rustlers. For a moment the Kid was quite alone, and he used that moment to stalk boldly toward the second cabin. Halfway there, he met the returning Felipe.

"It ees loco, *señor*," Felipe observed with a flash of his white teeth. "Why

176

should I feed thees prisoner hombres when tomorrow we keel them perhaps?"

"It's shore crazy," the Kid agreed, and laid his gun-barrel across Felipe's head.

The Mexican went down without a moan. Instantly the Kid was dipping into Felipe's pockets, and when he sprinted toward the dark prison-cabin, the key was in his hand. He thought he heard hoofs drumming in the distance, but he paid no heed. There wasn't time to be concerned about anything but the job that lay ahead.

He got the door open quickly enough. "Tara!" he whispered. "It's me — Matt!"

She came to the door at once, the others crowding at her back. "Matt!" she cried.

"You've got to work fast," he whispered. "They think I'm joining up with them, but I can't stay here long or I may be missed. You and the boys slip outa here and over to the corral and get gear onto horses. Work quiet — but work fast! I'll join you just as soon as I can. Then we'll make a break for it! Doesn't look like I'll have a chance to get guns for you."

A voice raised in the darkness. "Dusty! Hey, Dusty South!" it called stridently. "Where the hell are yuh? Cisco wants yuh!"

"I've got to go!" the Kid panted. "If they come lookin' and find me here, the game's up. I'll see what Cisco wants and stall him. Do like I said, meantime!"

He slid away, stepping over the body of Felipe, a shapeless huddle in the darkness. The man was still unconscious, and there was a prayer in the heart of the Gospel Kid that Felipe would stay unconscious for quite a while. Also that the cook wouldn't be missed by the others. The Kid walked boldly toward the lighted cabin, and big Cisco Yawberry was waiting for him just outside the door.

"Step inside, Dusty," Yawberry grinned. "The boss is here. I told him we had a new gent, but you can speak your own piece. Come on in and meet him."

The Kid remembered those drumming hoofbeats then. The rustler chief had arrived! That complicated things, but the Kid's cue was obvious. He had to stall all of them — the boss included — until Tara and Banty Ryan and Ike Tonkin and the Denny twins were in saddle.

So the Kid stepped into the cabin — stepped inside to stare slack-jawed at the man who'd just arrived. And if there was amazement in the Kid's eyes, it was mirrored in the eyes of the man he faced. For the boss of the rustling crew was Hoyt Durham of the Golden Slipper Saloon.

13.

Hoyt Durham! There was no mistaking the dandified, swarthy saloon-owner, even though Durham was a mighty long way from his usual stamping grounds. Of all the thoughts that flashed through the mind of the Gospel Kid as he faced the man there in the rustlers' lair, two were predominant. One was that Durham's presence in that place definitely branded the man as one of The Three. Durham was the leader of these night-riding raiders, which proved that the man was battling the Montana-Pacific for his own selfish gain.

The Kid's other thought, the uppermost at the moment, was that the game of bluff was definitely over. He wasn't going to fool Durham as he'd fooled Yawberry. Durham had known the Kid the first day in Caprock, for the saloon-owner had tried to have him killed that day. And now Durham was here.

So were all the others, except Felipe. Yawberry had stepped into the cabin. So had the man who'd called the Kid away from the prisoners. Most of the men ringed the table where cards were spread in the glow of a kerosene lamp — Shark Lund glowering in sullen silence, Cisco Yawberry grinning expectantly, the others merely waiting. But in another second Durham would speak, denounce this new recruit as an impostor, and the pack would be upon the Kid.

The Kid didn't wait for Durham to find his tongue. Instead, he kicked over the table. At the same time he swung at Durham, his fist lashing as the table crashed and the lamp blotted out to leave the room in darkness. He heard Durham sprawl across the wrecked table, and he heard men curse as they were pinned beneath the wreckage. Then the Kid was through the doorway.

"Dusty!" Yawberry was bellowing in stunned confusion. "What the hell — ?"

The Kid had forced the play and thereby gained the advantage of surprise. No man except Hoyt Durham had expected him to make a hostile move, and even Durham had obviously been unprepared for the Kid's lightning attack. Thus the Kid was able to get outside unscathed. He swung the door shut behind him, but instead of bolting into the darkness, he grasped the crude door handle and braced one foot against the cabin wall to hold the door shut.

"Tara!" he shouted over his shoulder. "Pile into saddles and git! Hell's busted loose!"

Cursing men were tugging at the door from the inside. There were eight of them, providing Durham hadn't been knocked unconscious, but no more than one or two of them could get their hands on the small inside handle at the same time. They couldn't combine their strength against the Kid's, so it required no great effort to keep them imprisoned.

But one of the rustlers, cooler-headed than the others, was driving bullets through the door, the lead smashing dangerously close to the Kid. That would be Shark Lund, probably. It would only be a matter of time until someone would have the presence of mind to climb through a window. All that the Kid could hope to do was to stall them for a few more precious minutes.

Would a few minutes be enough? Could Tara and the others complete their preparations for a getaway in that time, the Kid wondered desperately? The chances were that he couldn't hold out much longer. But now a horsebacker flashed by him — Tara Herndon.

"Up!" she shouted, and the Kid saw other riders, the Deadman cowpokes, fanning wide. They'd all gotten into saddle! The Kid let the door go, firing twice into the dark interior of the shack as the door swung inward. That lead stopped the first rush of men to the outside, and the Kid swung up behind Tara's saddle.

"Gotta get my own hoss!" the Kid panted. "Can't ride double and outrun 'em! They'll be hot on the trail before we've reached the tunnel!"

But Tara, it seemed, had conceived an idea of her own. And suddenly the Kid saw the shape of it. She was loping, not toward the distant tunnel and its comparative safety, but straight toward the corralled beef herd. The Deadman riders were already there ahead of her, and Banty Ryan was shaking out a loop, dabbing it on the corral gate, snaking it open. The cattle, hungry and thirsty and irritable, charged into the open — the riders whooping and slapping sombreros against their chaps as they spread to flank them.

The herd needed little urging. It smelled water to the east, and it bolted in that direction, a myriad-legged juggernaut goaded by a single compelling purpose — to reach that water. The rustlers' cabin was directly in the path of the herd, and the Kid saw Tara's strategy then. With a wild shout he fired a couple of shots to add to the bedlam, just as a half-dozen shadowy figures poured from the cabin.

Finding themselves facing that oncoming avalanche of beef, the rustlers stopped in their tracks. "Gawd!" one of them shrilled. With wild cries of terror they turned, dashing back to the shelter of the cabin's interior, piling up in the doorway, as anxious to close the door between themselves and death as they'd been to wrench it open.

One of them tripped, went down, then managed to struggle to his feet again. Too late! The Kid had a brief glimpse of the fear-twisted face of Shark Lund, saw the man's upflung arms as though the rustler were appealing to a Deity he'd long since forsaken. His wail of terror was like something from the realm of the lost. Then Lund vanished from view, submerged beneath a waving, tossing sea of horns as the herd split, surging around the cabin where the other rustlers cowered, safe enough but helpless.

Chick Denny had turned all of the

horses out of the little corral, and the mounts of the rustlers were swept along by the herd. Behind the racing animals came the Kid and his friends. In this manner they reached the inner mouth of the tunnel, and there the six in saddles sweated to force the fringe of the herd into the cavern, a herculean task for the steers jammed up against the inner cliff. It took patience and skill and a great deal of time.

Once that chore was done, the bulk of their work was over. Soon the herd was scattered along the stream, drinking its fill. Some of the steers had been crippled in the jam, and these the Kid had put out of their misery. Now he sat his saddle, gun in hand, his eye on the tunnel's mouth. But none of the rustlers put in an appearance, and shortly afterwards, the herd was rounded up and headed south by east.

"Might just as well push 'em on to-night," the Kid decided. "We don't have to worry about those galoots back yonder. They can't catch us without hosses. And there's no use tryin' to go back and round up those gents, either. They've got guns a-plenty. We've got one between the bunch of us — mine."

But first they angled to the site of their camp of the night before. The moon was soaring above the eastern rim of the prairie when they reached it, and there was light enough for the task that had to be done.

A shovel, used to bury the big Dutch oven which was part of the H-in-a-Hat's cooking equipment, had been fetched in the wagon. The Denny twins spelled each other with the shovel, and on the very spot where Dave Woods had died, a grave was dug for the valiant Flying V puncher.

Ike Tonkin and Banty Ryan had wrapped the body in a tarp. As it was lowered, Tara turned to the Kid.

"You still have Hank's Bible with you?" she asked.

He nodded, fumbling at his shirt-front. While the others stood bare-headed around the shallow grave, he flipped the pages to Revelations. " 'And God shall wipe away all tears from their eyes;' " he intoned, " 'and there shall be no more death, neither sorrow, nor crying, neither shall there be any more pain: for the former things are passed away.' "

He closed the Book, groping for words of his own. "I didn't know this gent very well," he said haltingly. "But I know that just for a little while him and me was tryin' to do the same job. Only it happened that there was a bullet with his name on it."

He glanced down into the grave. "This is about as much as we can do for you now, mister," he said. "It's adios. But maybe there'll be a time when I'll cross trails again with the bunch that was triggerin' here last night. When that time comes, Dave; I'll be rememberin' . . ."

At his nod, Chick Denny picked up the shovel. The Kid stowed the Bible back in his shirt-front. "We better be ridin' as quick as we can," he observed, and unconsciously glanced toward the west. "The time to cross trails with Yawberry's bunch wouldn't be *now*."

Dawn found them to the south, at the camp of the Montana-Pacific's tunnel builders. Since the railroad tunnel was nearly completed, the Kid took half a dozen workers from the crew and ordered them to help the Deadman riders guard the herd to the end of steel.

"Little chance you'll be bothered," the Kid explained to the railroad men. "But as long as you boys will be heading that way anyway, an extra guard won't hurt."

He toyed with the notion of taking another crew and heading back to the hidden valley to round up Yawberry's bunch. But that would just be a waste of time, he decided. With the valley's location no longer a secret, the rustler crew would have already gotten out of the hideout as fast as feet could carry them.

Tara had retired to a tent to snatch a few hours sleep, and she arose before the following noon to find the herd gone and the Kid waiting for her.

"You're going back to the H-in-a-Hat," he told her firmly. "I'll rep for your dad when the beef's paid for. You've done enough trail drivin' for one season, and I'm takin' you home."

She didn't argue. Those last two days had taken their toll of her, but if the smile she gave him was wan, it was also appreciative. Within an hour they were loping across the rangeland toward the distant H-in-a-Hat, two pygmy figures in that vast stretch of prairie. They talked of many things as they rode along, but mostly of Hellvation Hank, for the Kid was hungry for details about the brother he'd scarcely known.

"You're so different from him — yet like him too," Tara said. "Last night, when we buried poor Dave, you might have been Hank with the Book in your hand. You could hang up your gun and be a sky pilot, Matt."

He smiled at the thought. "I've studied

the Bible a heap," he admitted. "But that was to read some meaning into a message Hank left behind him. It's a queer yarn. . . ."

And then he found himself telling her the whole story of how he'd received that bloodstained Bible and had gradually come to understand the significance of the marked references. He explained how he'd taken the trail to the north then, and he told her of the things he'd learned since he'd gone to work for the railroad.

". . . Goliath, Herod, and Judas," he concluded thoughtfully. "I'm sure, now, that Bottsinger is Goliath. They tell me he stands to lose much when the railroad offers a cheaper service to take the place of his highway-robbin' freight line. And Hoyt Durham is Herod. If I had any doubts, they went up in smoke when Durham showed up last night. But Judas is the gent I've still got to cut sign on."

She'd listened in fascinated silence. "And when you do?" she ventured.

"Like you said — I'm different from Hank," he reminded her. He was grim enough as he said it to make her drop the subject.

Dusk was stealing across the rangeland when they reached the H-in-a-Hat, a cluster of buildings cupped in a verdant coulee to shelter them from the winds of winter. It was a pretty place, this H-in-a-Hat, with its barns and corrals and reservoir, a cowman's dream. Looking upon it for the first time, it came to the Kid that there could be no better ending to any trail than such a spread as this.

"There's Dad, waiting on the gallery!" the girl cried excitedly. "He'll want to meet you."

Storm Herndon was seated in a rocker on the long gallery that fronted the frame ranch-house. In the graying twilight the man and the girl were almost upon him before the Kid could really see the rancher. He was anxious to meet Storm Herndon, was the Kid, for he'd heard enough about the salty old cattleman to know he was going to like him. But when he gazed upon the sturdy oldster with the seamed, leathery face, with a ragged rim of gray hair fringing a semi-bald head, the Kid stiffened in his saddle with astonishment.

"Howdy," he said quietly. "We've met before, haven't we?"

"Dad!" Tara cried. "You'll never guess who this is! He's —"

Storm Herndon had half risen from his chair. He settled back again, his eyes aflame with anger as he glared at the Kid. Something about the rancher's wild look locked the tongue of his daughter.

"*You!*" Herndon suddenly roared. "Git out! Git off this place, mister! Do you savvy? Git off before I put a slug intuh you!"

Tara gazed in bewilderment from one man to the other. "Dad! You don't understand! This man —"

"It's you that don't savvy, gal," her father raged. "But you'll hate this hairpin as much as I do when you get the straight of it. Now git, mister, and git fast!"

The girl's eyes swung toward the Kid, and it was the anguish in them that held the Kid's tongue.

"Never mind," was all he said. Touching spurs to his horse, he rode out of the ranch yard. In this manner he turned his back upon the man he'd fought in Crowfoot Gulch the night he'd witnessed the dynamiting of the trestle — the man he'd last seen rolling down the slope of the gulch!

He heard Tara call after him, bewilderment in her voice, but he paid her no heed. He wanted to put distance between himself and the H-in-a-Hat to be alone so he could think things out. For there was plenty to think about!

Storm Herndon — dynamiter! That didn't make sense. Yet the rancher had certainly been in the gulch that night, and at this, their second meeting, he'd flared at sight of the Kid — the one man who knew he'd been there. That cinched Herndon's guilt, but still the Kid didn't want to believe the obvious. Yet Tyler Whitman himself had warned the Kid that Herndon might not be an ally.

"He hates the railroad and makes no bones about it . . ." Whitman had said, among other things. "If Herndon's got it into his head to buck the road, he'll fight hard . . ."

Did Storm Herndon hate the railroad so much that he was fighting it tooth and toenail, using any means at hand? It looked like it. The railroad was being welcomed by most ranchers, but Herndon was a diehard of another era, a man who wanted to cling to the old days and the old ways.

Yet Tara had been on the train which would have plunged into Crowfoot Gulch if the Kid hadn't stopped it! No man would endanger his own daughter. The Kid seized upon that thought until another came to cancel it. Had Herndon known that Tara was on that train?

And what about the fact that hirelings of

The Three had run off a beef herd belonging to Deadman ranchers? Yet that herd had been jointly owned by six spreads. Had Herndon included his own cattle in the herd in order to keep suspicion from himself? Had he allowed his daughter to go with the herd, knowing that no matter how much lead might be scattered, she'd be left unscathed?

Tara had appeared to be in danger of her life as a prisoner in the hidden valley. But where was the proof that she'd actually been in peril? Perhaps she would have been spared, no matter what happened to Banty Ryan and Ike Tonkin and the Denny twins. Not because she was a woman, but because she was Storm Herndon's girl.

There were a lot of things the Kid didn't know. But there were certainly signs that Storm Herndon might be betraying the other ranchers of Deadman range — and betraying his one-time friendship with Tyler Whitman.

At least there was no indication that Tara was aware of her father's perfidy. The Kid found some consolation in that as he wrestled with the riddle across the lonely miles, finding himself no nearer a solution when he unlimbered himself from his saddle in Lazura the next day.

192

His first duty was to report to Tyler Whitman. But before he sought the railroad builder, he went to the telegraph office. Key O'Dade had been moved from Caprock to this new boomtown, and the Kid found the squat Irishman at his clacking instrument.

"Look," said the Kid. "Can you dig something out of the records for me! I've got to know if Storm Herndon got a wire from his girl in April — a wire saying she'd be coming into Caprock on a certain train."

O'Dade scratched his head. "Shure and this is a railroad telegraph, and it's records we keep on railroad messages. Sich wires as we send for other folks is for the promotin' of good will along the right o' way. There's no record of thim, bhoy."

"But can't you remember?" the Kid urged desperately. "Think hard!"

O'Dade's red face corrugated with the effort. "I'm thinkin' there was no sich wire, but it's no oath I'll be takin' on it," he decided. "Things was opening up in April, and it's busy the wires was in thim days. No, bhoy, I can't tell you for sure."

The Kid turned into the clamorous street, his face grim. He'd hoped there'd be proof that Storm Herndon had known his daughter was coming on the train that might have been doomed. But there was no proof — nothing to dispel the black shadow of suspicion that clouded the Kid's mind. All the sign said Storm Herndon was an enemy of the railroad, a far more ruthless enemy than he admitted he was, a betrayer of his neighbors and his friend — a Judas.

It looked, the Kid observed grimly, as though he'd found his third man. But where was the satisfaction in that when the third man was Tara's father?

14.

Tyler Whitman, the Kid learned upon making inquiry, was still in Lazura. The Kid found the railroad builder in his private coach which sat upon a siding. Kurt Ormond was also there, in from the end of steel for some sort of conference with his superior, and both men greeted the Kid when he stepped through the doorway.

"So you're back, Matt," Whitman observed. "Which means that the railroad beef has been safely delivered."

"The herd's probably at end of steel right now," the Kid said. "I took the liberty of tollin' off some of the tunnel building crew to help haze it in. Seein' as the tunnel is so near bein' finished, and ahead of time at that, I figgered it would be O.K."

Whitman nodded. "Good enough," he conceded. "But seeing as you were taking extra precautions to guard the beef, I presume you ran into trouble of some sort."

"Rustlers stampeded the herd and ran it off," the Kid reported. "The Deadman boys who were reppin' for the herd trailed them to their hideout, and I tagged along afterwards. You see, I'd been nighthawkin' and I had a little accident that put me asleep about the time the fun started. What happened at the hideout is neither here nor there. The main point is that we managed to get away and take the herd with us. But that wasn't until after the boss of the night riders showed up and I had a look at him."

"The boss — ?"

"Hoyt Durham," said the Kid.

Tyler Whitman's brows raised. "Durham!" he echoed. "You really got the deadwood on him — caught him bucking us red-handed?"

"He's buckin' us all right," the Kid assured him. "No mistake about that. I guess rustlin' is nothing new on Deadman range, but Durham's wide-loopin' boys seem to have a special craving for railroad beef."

Whitman frowned, drumming his fingertips on the top of the table which served as his desk, his eyes thoughtful as he digested this piece of information.

"The question now is what are we going to do about it?" he said at last. "There isn't any law here in Lazura, so we can't have him arrested. Besides, he'd probably deny all the charges. It would only be your word against his, Matt. If we could catch him at his dirty work, like we caught that fellow in Crowfoot Gulch the night Hanson was murdered, we might give Durham the same kind of medicine. But this is a different sort of situation."

He shot a glance at his still-faced lieutenant. "What do you think about it, Kurt?" he asked.

The chief engineer shrugged. "I was against our taking the law into our own hands at Crowfoot Gulch that night," Ormond said. "I'm still against it. That sort of thing only gives the railroad a bad name, even when the circumstances justify rope law. As it is, about all we can hope to gain from what McGrath discovered is the certain knowledge that Durham is our enemy. I imagine Durham will be a lot more careful from now on. He'll probably lay low for a while, just as Bottsinger has been laying low since the day that McGrath exposed him as an agitator and beat him up."

But Whitman had obviously been turning the matter over in his mind meanwhile. "Wait!" he cried, his eyes lighting with inspiration. "I can hit back at Durham! And I can hit him where it will hurt the worst — in his pocketbook. I'll post an order that no M.P. man is to patronize his place. I'll blacklist him, drive him out of business."

"It might work," Ormond ruminated dubiously.

"But you know how it is with the men, chief. They'd resent any infringement upon their personal liberty. The Golden Slipper has always been the most popular saloon. That kind of an order would be a little out of line and —"

"There should be an off-shift crew in town right now," the Kid interjected, for the idea had seized his fancy. "Most of 'em will probably be down at the Golden Slipper. Want to try givin' it a whirl, Whitman?"

"Why not?" the railroad builder decided, and came to his feet. Kurt Ormond shook his head doubtfully, but he trailed after his chief. With Matt McGrath striding along beside Whitman, the three of them headed into the town. The heat of June laid its sweltering hand upon Lazura, but the weight of it did not keep the flow of humanity from the boardwalks. Elbowing through the press of men, the three came at last to the Golden Slipper.

Inside, they found the place packed. The

Kid, busy at the end of steel or out upon the range for many days past, hadn't been in the new Golden Slipper before. Flimsy though it was, made for transporting from one town to another as the rails pushed westward, it was much like the saloon the Kid had visited in Caprock.

Yonder stood the very bar where he had drunk with Shadow Loomis, and behind it ran the same mirror that had given him a glimpse of that seedy-looking man pouring his drink into a cuspidor. "The Lady of the Nile" smiled down upon him, and the Kid remembered that once he'd thought he'd detected a semblance of life in the picture. And oddly, at the memory a fear stirred him.

Somehow he'd hardly expected to find Hoyt Durham here. True, the man had had time enough to get back from Hidden Valley, granting that he and Yawberry's bunch had been able to get horses from some dubious source. But the Kid had guessed that Durham might not be anxious to show his face in town so soon. Yet Durham was here, bejeweled and dandified as ever. He leaned against his own bar, a purple welt on his swarthy face showing where the Kid's fist had marked him in the rustlers' cabin.

Durham stiffened perceptibly as the three railroad men paused just within the batwings. The Kid gave him a speculative glance but made no other sign that he was aware of the saloon-owner's presence. This was Tyler Whitman's show, the Kid had decided. Let Whitman make whatever play he chose to make. The Kid was merely along to back that play.

The saloon was thronged with men, most of them in various stages of intoxication. It was a motley aggregation of humanity that liquored there, but the majority of the drinkers were Montana-Pacific workmen who instantly recognized the three in the doorway. Patently they were surprised to see Whitman there. The name of the railroad builder passed through the room, becoming a whisper and then the ghost of a whisper. On the heels of the silence that fell then, Tyler Whitman raised his voice.

"Most of you boys work for me," Whitman said without prelude. "What you do with your pay or your own time is no concern of mine. But we've just gotten certain proofs that the man who runs this establishment is an enemy of M.P. It happens that there isn't much we can do about it. But I'm asking every man of you to stay out of this place, to spend your money elsewhere. Is that asking too much?"

Boots shuffled restlessly as the little speech ended. Amazement, disbelief, scorn and respect — all these things were in the faces that were turned toward Whitman. One laborer, his face flushed with liquor, spoke first. "By God, do we gotta ask him if we can blow our noses?" he demanded.

That was all the encouragement Hoyt Durham needed. Obviously he hadn't been prepared for Tyler Whitman's speech, but he knew how to counteract it, for he'd just been given a cue. Leaping to the nearest chair, he stood upon it, his hands upraised.

"Whitman can't do this!" he protested. "Don't listen to him, gents. He says I'm an enemy of Montana-Pacific. That's a lie! I happen to know that he's personally invested money in another of the saloons here in Lazura. He wants the railroad trade to go to it. What kind of men are you, anyway? You've got minds of your own! And your money is your own, once you've earned it. Tell him to go to hell! You're the ones that can be giving out the orders, not him. He couldn't lay another foot of steel without you!"

"Thash right!" the drunk who had first

spoken yelled. "We drink where we damn please!"

Anything might have happened then. Tyler Whitman had made his plea, and, from the looks of things, the plea was going unheeded. And Whitman knew his own limitations. He could only ask; he couldn't command in a matter of this sort. At the Kid's side, Ormond groaned.

"I told you —" he began.

And that was when the Kid took matters into his own hands, for a plan had been shaping itself while he'd been listening to Durham's tirade.

"Just a minute," he cried, his voice loud enough to draw every eye to him. "Your big boss has just asked you boys to do something, as a favor to him. Durham, there, tells you you don't have to do it. And he's right — you don't. It's all up to you. But I'm willin' to make a sportin' proposition out of it. Let me and Durham fight it out. He's too runty to go matchin' fists with me, so it can be any other kind of a fight he wants. If Durham wins, you boys keep on spendin' your money here as long as you please. No more will be said about it. But if I win, you do as Mr. Whitman asked you to do. Now what do you say?"

This was the sort of proposition that

would appeal to these workers as nothing else would. And the Kid knew it. They might rebel against what they considered an unjust order, but they could appreciate anything that smacked of a gamble or a fight. Here were both of those things rolled into one!

Also, they were willing to listen to the Kid. Tyler Whitman was their superior. But Whitman, with a thousand jobs to do, had never had the opportunity to make personal contact with the rank and file of his men. But the Kid was one of them — a fighting man who'd proved his prowess, the man who'd beaten Bottsinger. The Kid had just appealed to them in their own language. Even the rebellious drunk changed from truculence to enthusiasm.

"A fight!" he chortled happily. "Let the besh man win. We'll back the winner, eh, boysh!"

"Does that sound fair enough to you, Durham?" the Kid asked.

Durham's face was black with wrath, but he could hardly hesitate when he had no choice. "Figure it's a cinch, eh, McGrath?" he spat. "Remember — you granted me the say as to how we'll fight! I know how you can handle a gun, and I know what you can do with your fists. But let's see how you stack up against something that isn't exactly in your line. I'm meaning a knife!"

"A knife!" the Kid echoed scornfully. "I don't pack one."

Durham dipped one bejeweled hand beneath the knee-length plantation-style coat he wore, and produced a glittering knife with an ornate handle. "Give this loud-mouth a blade," he ordered a bartender.

Whitman, his face ashen, tugged at the Kid's elbow. "You don't have to go through with this, Matt," he whispered hoarsely. "Call it off! If it was a white man's kind of fight, I wouldn't care!"

A knife was slid across the bar, a formidable-looking blade if not a fancy one. The Kid looked at it, something cold forming in the pit of his stomach. Down along the Rio, every Mexican was likely to have such a weapon. The Kid was no stranger to a knife, but he had a gringo's scorn for such a weapon and a natural aversion to what a blade could do to a man. But —

"*Get at it!*" he said with a vast disgust, and picked up the blade.

Durham slipped off his coat to allow freer movement of his arms. Draping the coat across the bar, he placed his flat-crowned black sombrero on top of it. "A new game for you, McGrath?" he grinned. "The rules are very simple. There aren't any. But you've got to win by a knife thrust. No fists, remember!"

Then Durham was lunging toward him, his knife flashing as it arced upward. Instantly the crowd was spreading itself against the walls and against the bar, kicking gaming tables out of the way to leave a cleared space for the combatants. And across that space Durham came charging, his face a cold mask.

The Kid met him halfway, instinctively trying to parry Durham's downward driving blade with his own knife. But Durham's wrist dropped, and the man dived under the Kid's arm while the Kid's weapon whistled through the air. The Kid side-stepped, and none too quickly. He heard cloth rip as Durham's knife sliced through his shirt, and he felt the trickle of blood as the skin was pricked over his ribs.

The Kid went dancing backwards out of harm's way, but Durham was after him. Desperately the Kid flicked his knife in a motion that menaced Durham's midriff, and the saloon-owner instantly lowered his own blade to parry the thrust. Quick as a darting snake the Kid sent his blade flashing upward toward Durham's shoulder. But Durham was not to be caught napping quite so easily. Writhing aside, the saloon-owner suffered little more than a scratch as the Kid's knife grazed him in passing, and he grinned wolfishly at the Kid's chagrin.

He was an old hand at this game, was Durham. That was obvious. With the fight scarcely started, the Kid was beginning to feel the same fear he'd had the day he'd fought Curly Bottsinger — the fear that it was going to be a great deal harder to finish this fight than it had been to start it. But at least he had the shadow of hope. Amateur though he was at this sort of fighting, he was learning the rudiments quickly — learning them the hard way.

It was something like fist fighting, the Kid decided. You guarded against the other fellow's blows, and at the same time, you tried to get in a few licks for yourself. Footwork and feinting helped too; but there the similarity ended. Putting power behind a blow didn't necessarily make that blow more effective in this kind of fighting. Striking hard might throw a man off balance. This sort of game went to the wily, not to the strong.

Durham was wily enough. He gave the

Kid many bad moments, drawing blood twice as often as the trouble-shooter did. Yet neither of them had gotten in anything approximating a vital blow, though the Kid was beginning to suspect that Durham might do so at any time, if he chose. It looked as though the saloon-owner were playing cat-and-mouse and enjoying every minute that he prolonged the affair.

The Kid was hard pressed, and now his breath was coming laboriously, and sweat was making his hand slippery. The summer sun, beating down upon the saloon's roof, seemed to have an intensity to it that made the barroom a furnace. He was aware that the crowd was shouting advice and encouragement, but to him it was only a meaningless babble of sound, just as the endless roar from the street had become distant as though the world had narrowed down to this little cleared space where he and Durham fought.

Durham's flashing blade seemed to be everywhere at once. White teeth gleamed as Durham grinned in satisfaction, and always the man's swarthy face swam before the Kid. Once the Kid slipped and went down to his knees. Instantly Durham was towering over him, blade upraised. "No rules!" Durham had said. The Kid rolled across the floor, and came to his feet in time to meet the saloon-owner's charge. His own blade flashed, striking blindly at the other.

But disaster guided the knife of the Gospel Kid. He had come to his feet near one of the posts that supported the ceiling, and his blade sank deep into the wood. With a hoarse chuckle of triumph, Durham closed in upon him. Wrenching savagely, the Kid hauled away at the imbedded knife. The sound that reached his ears was like the crack of doom. The blade had snapped off!

A defective knife! The Kid understood then. He'd been given a blade that Durham must have kept handy for just such occasions as this — a blade that had been tampered with so that it would become useless the moment it was really put to a test. So far the Kid had never locked blades with Durham. But by striking the post he'd done as much damage, for now he was weaponless.

Here was a piece of treachery entirely consistent with the ways of Hoyt Durham. But what good was that knowledge when Durham was almost upon him, his arm upraised, his eyes glittering with the lust to kill? Before him stood the Kid, the useless knife in his hands. There was a throaty bellow from the crowd, evidence enough that some had seen what had happened to the Kid's knife — and understood. But the crowd couldn't help the Kid in the split second that was left before he'd go down.

Instinct, then, was his only ally at the moment. "No rules," Durham had decreed. "But you've got to win by a knife thrust. No fists, remember!"

Shaking the sweat from his eyes, the Kid discarded his useless knife and clawed for Durham's right wrist, his fingers closing just beneath the saloon-owner's blade. Twisting hard, the Kid lunged against Durham. It happened faster than an eye could follow, but Durham sagged to the floor, screaming in pain. The Kid had turned Durham's blade and, before the man could comprehend the Kid's intent and drop the knife, Matt had plunged Durham's own blade into the saloon-owner's shoulder.

Methodically the Kid kicked the bloody blade across the floor. Then he stood panting over the fallen man. "Had enough, you double-dealin' snake?" he demanded.

Durham's only answer was a moan. The Kid lifted his eyes to the white-faced crowd, a soberer bunch of men than they had been a few minutes before. "Satisfied?" he asked.

For answer, a man started toward the batwings. Another paced at his heels. In groups they marched outside and away, the men of the Montana-Pacific. And the Kid knew that though the manner of his victory hadn't been exactly what had been expected, still the victory had indeed been accepted for what it was.

Without another glance at Durham, the Kid walked from the saloon, Whitman and Ormond flanking him. A silence held between the three until they were once again in Whitman's private coach. There Ormond extended his hand, a grin breaking the inscrutability of his face. "I'll say this much for you, McGrath," the engineer said, genuine admiration in his eyes. "You're an all-around fighting man! And you're all for the railroad. I'm sorry I ever doubted you."

The Kid grinned in return. "That makes two fights I won today," he observed.

They stripped away his shirt, finding no serious cuts, but Ormond insisted on going after the railroad doctor who was in Lazura. After the engineer had left, Tyler Whitman extended his hand.

"I'm mighty grateful to you, Matt," he

said. "You did what I wouldn't have been able to do. The last Montana-Pacific payroll dollar has crossed the bar of the Golden Slipper. I'm thinking Durham was lucky our boys didn't pull his place down over his head after they realized how he nearly tricked you to your death with that faulty knife."

"Losin' the railroad trade will hit Durham just as hard as if they did," the Kid grunted.

"By the way, Matt," Whitman added, "did you finish your report before we went down to the saloon? Was there anything else you wanted to say about the rustling of that beef herd?"

Anything else? There'd been no word said about Storm Herndon, who'd proved to be the man who'd been in Crowfoot Gulch the night of the dynamiting. Now was the time to report to Whitman that he, the Kid, had unmasked another deadly enemy of the Montana-Pacific. Suddenly the Kid found himself having trouble meeting the eyes of his superior. He passed a hand before his own eyes wearily.

"The details don't matter," said the Kid. "I've told you everything you need to know."

15.

The steel reached Deadman the second week in July, rejuvenating the torpid town the Kid had seen when his trail had taken him there weeks before. With hammers pounding day and night, a score of buildings blossomed to lengthen the false-fronted street, for hard on the heels of the advancing railroad came the horde that followed the steel. Deadman had accepted the heritage of turmoil bequeathed by a dying Lazura and a dead Caprock.

On the last day of July the rails were twenty miles beyond Deadman. The Big Thunders echoed to a thousand alien sounds, the clang of sledge against spike, the puff and rattle of work trains. For the Montana-Pacific, its first tunnel completed and waiting, had passed the beginning of the mountain barrier without a wasted day.

The Gospel Kid was always at end o' steel these blazing days, working as he'd never worked before. Under the blistering sun he was everywhere and anywhere, sometimes pumping a handcar up and down the right of way, alert for trouble that scarcely ever materialized, sometimes swinging a sledge or lending a hand when the track-layers deposited the shining steel upon the ladder of ties that climbed a ways toward the west.

He was a troubled man, was the Kid; a man who found his waking hours a torture and who worked ceaselessly so that he might find sleep and forgetfulness when night came. He grew lean and morose and his easy grin was gone. There was no enthusiasm in him, even though each day brought victory nearer for the Montana-Pacific. Rumor whispered that Central Western was so far behind as to be almost out of the race.

In early June, when the Kid had come back from Deadman range after the delivery of the beef herd, he'd added only one piece of information to his report to Tyler Whitman. "Herndon's gal was along with the herd, reppin' for her dad's H-in-a-Hat," the Kid had said. "After that fracas with the rustlers, I took her back home."

"I'll send Herndon's money to him by one of the Deadman cowpokes," Whitman had promised.

It was the last that was ever said about the matter, but therein lay the reason for the Kid's turmoil. It was his duty to tell Whitman the whole story, including his suspicions concerning Storm Herndon. And it was the Kid's duty — to himself — to force a showdown with Hoyt Durham, since the Kid was satisfied in his own mind that Durham was one of The Three.

True, he'd fought the man in the Golden Slipper and wounded him, though not badly, the Kid had learned later. But that had been part of Matt McGrath's job as trouble-shooter for the Montana-Pacific, an impersonal chore that had had to be done in order to back up Tyler Whitman's plan to squeeze Durham out of business.

No, that wasn't the sort of showdown the Kid had promised himself when he'd taken the trail north from Texas to uncover the identity of three men. He hadn't seen Hoyt Durham since the day of the knife fight, and he hadn't run into big Curly Bottsinger either, for the simple reason that the Kid chose to avoid the pair — and hated himself for doing it.

But the Kid was beaten — beaten by a slip of a girl with dark hair and blue eyes, a girl who came no higher than his chin. He was honest enough to face the fact. He'd sworn to kill three men, men who were like Goliath and Herod and Judas. But one was as guilty as the others. Yet if his torturing suspicions were true and Tara Herndon's father was Judas, how could he kill the rancher? And what could he say before the tribunal of his own conscience if he wreaked vengeance upon Hoyt Durham and Curly Bottsinger and spared the third man?

Such a fine point of ethics might not have troubled Matt McGrath of the Rio. But the Gospel Kid had learned to see things in a different light. Exactly what change had come over him he did not know, nor did he seek to know. For necessity's sake he had studied Hellvation Hank's Bible, and, because he carried that Bible, he had been called upon to do Hellvation Hank's work from time to time. Those things had brought him a new sense of values. And loving Tara Herndon had done something, as well, to banish the old McGrath of the Rio forever.

In any case, the Kid's hands were tied now that vengeance might have been his. And that is why he worked like a demon, keeping himself going from morning to night, until he began to sense that a man may move swiftly but never so fast that he can escape from himself. But still he toiled on, with the heart gone out of him, until

Tyler Whitman, misunderstanding, called him aside on that last day of July.

"Are you trying to build this railroad single-handed, Matt?" he chided the Kid. "There's a limit to what one man can do, though you don't seem to realize it. The trouble we were having seems to be all over, and you've earned a rest. Take a couple days off and go into Deadman and have some fun. That's an order, understand."

The Kid didn't argue. There was no lure for him in Deadman, but he took the work train back to town, finding the blackness of the new tunnel en route no darker than his mood. He alighted to swing along another clamorous street, to see the same signs that had adorned Caprock and Lazura, to hear the same barkers shouting from a dozen saloon doorways.

He swung past the tent housing Thackery Weaver's transplanted *End O' Steel Echo*, quickening his pace as he heard the thunder of the press, for he was in no frame of mind to listen to the garrulous editor. When he came abreast of the Palace Hotel, he turned inside for want of a better place to spend his time.

The room he was given overlooked the alley. The Kid sat before the window, staring out with brooding eyes, the clamor of the street beating against him as it rose from the distance. He toyed with the idea of going on a good toot and was annoyed to find that such an idea no longer held any allure for him. And while he sat there, wrapped in his gloomy thoughts, he saw a figure steal surreptitiously down the alleyway below, and he instantly recognized the gaunt, seedy-looking man — Shadow Loomis.

The Kid's interest quickened. He'd never gotten any nearer than within shouting distance of Shadow Loomis since that day in Caprock when he'd bought liquor for Loomis — liquor which the man had poured into a cuspidor. But the Kid had thought of Shadow Loomis often and had wanted to talk to him. So now the Kid swung a leg over the window sill, dropped to the roof of a low shed flanking the rear of the hotel and leaped to the ground.

But now Loomis was nowhere to be seen. Five minutes before the Kid had been without a purpose. The sight of Loomis had shaped one, and suddenly it was the most important thing in the world that he find the man who pretended to be a barfly. He hurried into the alleyway, skipping nimbly over piled debris, and glimpsed the seedy-looking man just angling out of the far end of the alley. Swiftly and silently the Kid followed after him.

The trail of Shadow Loomis was a sinuous one, and sometimes the Kid was hard put to keep him in sight. Always the Kid stalked with caution, for he was remembering that two of The Three might be here in Deadman town. He was leaving them strictly alone, but they had no code to restrain them from turning an ambush gun upon him. But the Kid managed to keep an eye on Loomis, and he was still behind the man when Loomis scurried into a small shack on the outskirts of Deadman, a sagging-roofed structure so decrepit-looking as to be a fitting abode for the dissolute man.

Was this where Loomis lived in Deadman? Or had Loomis come here to meet someone else? When the Kid pressed an ear to the flimsy outer wall, he heard only the slight movements of one man inside. The Kid opened the door without knocking, and boldly stepped inside.

A crude table, a few crippled chairs, a cot, and a rusty, lopsided stove furnished the single room. Loomis was seated behind the table, and just for an instant astonishment crossed his face as he recognized the

Kid. Then his eyes grew as bleary as ever, and his voice held its whining note.

"What are you doing here?" he demanded with a faint show of truculence.

"I've come for a palaver," said the Kid, "and I ain't in a mood to mess with words. Just who the hell are you, mister, and what's your game?"

"Game? I'm just a gent who's down on his luck," Loomis countered, half cringing. "I'm not making trouble for anybody; honest I ain't."

"That's all you've got to say?"

"That's all," Loomis quavered.

The Kid swept the table aside with a brush of his hand. He was upon Loomis in the same motion, his fingers gripping the man's stringy throat.

"Talk, damn you!" the Kid gritted. "Talk up — and talk fast! You've followed the steel all the way from Caprock. You sneak and you snoop, and you're always around, and you ain't no part of what you pretend to be. Mister, I'm thinkin' you might be one of The Three!"

Loomis, gasping, managed to speak. "The Three!" he spluttered. "You figure — ?"

"I dunno," the Kid said truthfully, for suddenly he was a little ashamed of his own belligerence. True enough, this seedy-looking creature was a man of mystery; but where was the proof that he was also a man of evil? It came to the Kid that he himself was clutching at straws, looking in vain for another Judas when he'd already found the real one.

"Wait!" Loomis cried. "I'll show you how wrong you are." He scurried to his cot, groped under it, and dragged an object into view. "Look!" he said. "Do you still think I'm on *their* side of the fence?"

"Another one!" the Kid gasped. And all of the doubt went out of him, for Loomis held a headboard aloft, a pine headboard much like the one the Kid had seen in Dan Callishaw's room back in Caprock on the day that Dan Callishaw had died. The lettering read:

HERE LIES S. LOOMIS
Died August 15, 1889
HIS EARS WAS TOO BIG FOR
THE SIZE OF HIS HEAD

"August fifteenth!" the Kid cried. "Shucks, man, that's only a couple of weeks away! Just why have they put the deadwood on you, mister?"

Loomis, thrusting the headboard out of

sight again, regarded the Kid thoughtfully for a full minute. It was as though the mystery man were trying to reach a decision of some sort. The bleariness had gone out of his eyes, and his shoulders began to straighten.

"Maybe I'd better tell you the whole truth of it," he decided, and even his voice had changed, for the whining note was gone. "They're after me because they suspect what I really am. Here, feel —" He took the Kid's hand, pressing it against his shabby corduroy coat. The Kid felt the bulge of something sewed inside the lining.

"Government credentials," Loomis explained.

It was like being hit with a wagon tongue. "A government man!" the Kid exclaimed, his eyes widening. "You! Doing what?"

"Keeping an eye on the race between Montana-Pacific and Central Western. The government has promised to subsidize the first road to cross the Big Thunders. A bond issue and a gift of a couple hundred feet of right of way on both sides of the rails isn't to be sneezed at. But the government wants the race to be fair. I'm out here to watch things."

"But why didn't you let us know?" the

Kid demanded. "Why didn't you tell Tyler Whitman?"

"Those weren't my orders," Loomis explained. "I was told to work incognito, playing whatever sort of role I saw fit. My findings were to be kept to myself, reported to my superiors afterwards. I came to Caprock last fall, pretending to be some sort of drunken remittance man. That's how I met up with Hellvation Hank —"

"Then you did know Hank?"

Loomis smiled wryly. "Know him? He tried to save me from what he thought I was! He worked hard to keep me away from the whiskey I appeared to be drinking. Yes, I knew him — and respected him highly. Probably that's why I'm telling you all this. It was to Hank that I first spoke of The Three — something I had no business doing. But I made a slip, and he worked on me until I'd told him as much as I knew. The railroad meant a lot to Hank."

The Kid was all excitement. "You know the names of The Three?" he demanded.

"I know the identity of two of them," Loomis admitted. "Since I rather guess that M.P. also knows, there isn't any reason why I shouldn't speak the names of Hoyt Durham and Curly Bottsinger. I've never found out who the third man is. I heard the other two speak of him when they didn't know I was listening, but they never mentioned his name. I told Hank that much, and he did some snooping for himself. And he learned the whole truth, somehow, for he told me so. 'Come to church and perhaps you'll hear all three names,' he told me. It was that same night he died."

"But you've got your suspicions," the Kid said bluntly. "I'm askin' you, as one man to another — is Storm Herndon tied up with The Three, to your way of thinking?"

"I don't know," Loomis shrugged. "Honestly I don't. I managed to search Durham's private office once, but I couldn't find a thing to implicate any one person. Yet Herndon was in Caprock last fall, and this spring too. He's certainly done more talking against the railroad than any other one person. If I were trouble-shooter for M.P., McGrath, I'd have a talk with him and force his hand. Make him say exactly how he stands!"

"You're right," the Kid said slowly. "You're dead right! It's what I should have done in the first place. And it's what I'm going to do — right pronto!"

He hesitated, troubled by a new thought. "What about Thackery Weaver?" he asked. "Do you know anything about him, Loomis? He had a list of birth dates in his office, and I've always had a hunch that The Three used that list whenever they wanted to make up one of those wooden warnings. Weaver claims his list was stolen. But what else could he claim?"

"I'm afraid I can't help you," Loomis confessed. "Weaver is a queer sort of bird. But he's an old-timer. I'm told. And he was a friend of Hellvation Hank's, from all indications. No, I think you can scratch Thackery Weaver off your list. He has no reason to buck the railroad."

The Kid extended his hand, a ghost of his old grin crossing his face. "I'm sorry I mussed you up some," he said. "And thanks a heap for layin' your cards out on the table for me. Take care of yourself, mister. When them boys send you one of those timber tombstones, they ain't jokin'!"

"I know it," Loomis said soberly. "I'm fading from town for a couple of weeks, going to hole up in the Big Thunders. My work is really finished anyway. So long, McGrath. I'm asking that you keep what I told you under your sombrero. The information was for Hank McGrath's brother — not for the trouble-shooter of M.P."

"They're two different fellows — sometimes," the Kid conceded gravely, and left.

His destination was many miles away — the H-in-a-Hat spread. He was going to have a showdown with Storm Herndon, and he wondered why he hadn't gone and forced one before. The very decision lifted some of the load he'd been shouldering. But before he left Deadman, he went to the railroad office and found Key O'Dade, who was still following the steel. The Irishman greeted him gravely.

"Faith and it was looking for ye I was," he said. "This wire came from Whitman for ye. 'Tis bad news, me bhoy; bad news!"

The Kid ran his eye over the proffered slip. "WATCH YOUR BACK," Whitman had wired. "HEADBOARD SIMILAR TO ONE SENT CALLISHAW FOUND IN YOUR TENT STOP NAMES AUGUST SECOND AS DAY OF YOUR DEATH."

"August second," the Kid mused, and balled the slip in his fist. "Time enough to get to the H-in-a-Hat, anyway."

Ten minutes later he was swinging aboard a work train headed for end o' steel.

★ ★ ★

The Golden Slipper Saloon had come to Deadman with the dying of Lazura, a more substantial Golden Slipper than had existed in the last town. M.P.'s progress would be slower in the mountains, and rumor had it that Deadman might enjoy a boom until the following spring. But though the Golden Slipper was prepared to continue reaping the golden harvest, it was a silent, gloomy place, for the Gospel Kid had clinched a bargain and Montana-Pacific men shunned the establishment of Hoyt Durham.

At first Durham hadn't believed that the blacklisting would really take effect. He had come on to Deadman, confident that the railroad trade would filter back. But now he'd become convinced that he'd poured his money into an investment that would bring no returns, and some of his disgust showed in his swarthy face as he sat in his private office, situated, as always, behind that tricky painting, "The Lady of the Nile." A black mood was upon Curly Bottsinger, too, and the giant was voicing his pessimism.

"McGrath headed back for end o' steel," he reported. "One of the boys saw him catch the train. But that wooden warning ain't gonna scare that gent a damn' bit! And we're wastin' our time scarin' small fry like Shadow Loomis."

The third man was the only one in a buoyant mood. He smiled expansively.

"If Loomis is what I think he is, he isn't small fry," he observed. "If I'm wrong — what difference does it make what happens to a barfly? But remember, Loomis has asked a lot of questions around, and a heap of them had to do with The Three. And as far as McGrath is concerned, I didn't expect the headboard would scare him into running. On the contrary, it will keep him out at end o' steel for the next couple of days. He'll figure we'll strike where we left the warning — which is exactly what I want him to think. That means he won't be in Deadman to smell a rat when things begin to happen. He's been our stumbling block all along, and we mustn't slip this time. Do I make myself clear?"

Hoyt Durham, quicker of wit than the burly Bottsinger, was the first to understand. He smiled eagerly, all interest now. "You mean you're ready to pull the big act," he demanded, "the plan we prepared if everything else failed to stop M.P.? You figure the time has come for the real showdown?"

"Exactly," said the third man. "Didn't you say that Cisco Yawberry and his bunch will be sneaking into town just as soon as they finish that little business out on Deadman range? Fine! Yawberry will have his chore to do, and everybody else is ready. We've all got our work cut out for us. Remember, it's got to work like a clock!"

"It's come," Bottsinger murmured to himself. "It's finally come!"

The third man poured himself a drink from Durham's private bottle, and the other two followed suit. They hoisted their glasses together.

"To the downfall of Montana-Pacific," toasted the third man. "And to the greater glory of Central Western."

"To the hell that's gonna be turned loose!" Bottsinger added darkly, and downed his drink in a single gulp.

16.

When the Gospel Kid had first visited the H-in-a-Hat, the day he'd escorted Tara Herndon home, the spread had been northwest of the end o' steel. Now that Montana-Pacific had pushed to Deadman and beyond, the Herndon ranch was to the northeast of the grading camps. Yet the Kid rode the work train to the very end of the tracks.

He still burned with a desire to see Herndon, to rid himself of his festering suspicions or to force the old rancher to show his hand. Storm Herndon was going to have to admit or deny his enmity with the Montana-Pacific, and he was going to have to explain his presence in Crowfoot Gulch on the night of the trestle dynamiting. The Kid had determined to get the truth out of the man. But first the Kid wanted to see Tyler Whitman. He found the railroad builder in Whitman's private coach, which had been hauled to the end o' steel.

"I'm glad you came back!" Whitman said heartily, a worried frown wedging between his brows. "One of the boys poked into your tent for something or other and found that headboard not long after you'd left for town. I'd like to think it's a bluff, Matt; but I'm not so sure. They weren't bluffing when they sent that same kind of warning to Dan Callishaw, remember."

The headboard had been brought to the coach, and Whitman produced it now. The lettering read:

HERE LIES MATTHEW McGRATH
Born January 1, 1864
Died August 2, 1889
HE WAS LUCKY — BUT HIS LUCK RAN OUT

The Kid scarcely gave it a glance. His thoughts made him solemn, but they had nothing to do with that wooden warning.

"I'm quitting the railroad," he told Whitman. "No — I'm not runnin' out on account of that headboard. It ain't that. It's just that I sorta made a promise to Kurt Ormond once. I told him I had two jobs to do. I said that if it ever happened that I had to take care of the other job first, I'd leave the railroad. Looks like I've got some business of my own to tend to — important business. I'm takin' a little *pasear* across the range."

Whitman regarded him thoughtfully. "Have it your way, boy," he decided at last. "I'll ask no questions. And I'll feel better if you're somewhere else for a spell — especially on August second. But I want you to know that we've a place for you here whenever you finish this other job of yours. Good luck — and be careful!"

Ten minutes after they'd shaken hands, the Kid was in a saddle. He followed the rails back through the tunnel and beyond it, angling northward then. He made a fireless camp when night overtook him not far from the cliffs that barricaded Hidden Valley to the west of him.

Most of the day his mind had been upon what might happen at the end of this trail. It wasn't until he was stretched upon his saddle blanket, studying the canopy of stars overhead and smoking a last cigarette, that he was struck by a puzzling thought. His birth date, as lettered on the headboard, had been the correct date!

That was queer, mighty queer, the Kid decided. Dan Callishaw's birth date had been correct too, but Callishaw had given information to Thackery Weaver which the editor had used in his newspaper write-up about the trouble-shooter. Thus Callishaw's birth date had become a matter of

231

public knowledge.

On the other hand, Loomis' headboard had mentioned no birth date. But that was understandable too. Loomis, seemingly a barfly, hadn't been worthy of inclusion in the list of names and data Thackery Weaver had kept in his office — the list the editor had claimed had been stolen.

But no man in all the range stretching from Caprock to the Big Thunders had known the birth date of Matt McGrath, save Hellvation Hank, his brother. And Hank was dead. How the devil, the Kid wondered, had the ones who'd prepared that headboard known what date to letter upon it?

It was a riddle, and the Kid went to sleep trying to solve it. With morning he gave it no further thought. The miles were soon unreeling behind him, and he was nearing the lush coulee that sheltered the H-in-a-Hat buildings. Once again his mind was upon the things he was going to say to Storm Herndon when he faced that fiery cattleman.

The trail dipped into the coulee a mile below the ranchhouse. Here the ravine was narrower, thronged riotously with rose briars and service-berry bushes, the shrubbery forming a screen of sorts with the trail worming through it. It was here that the Kid rounded a turn to find himself facing an oncoming rider. His heart leaped at the sight, for it was Tara, dressed in the same levis and jumper and floppy sombrero she'd been wearing when he'd seen her last.

For a long moment they faced each other as each jerked to a halt. "Matt!" Tara cried then. "You've come back! I —" Something in his face, rocky and inscrutable, made her voice falter.

"I've come to see your father," he said. "Maybe you can guess why. But tell me one thing first, Tara — the thing I've *got* to know. Did you wire him that you were coming to Caprock by train last spring?"

"Wire him? No, I didn't. He'd told me to stay East, and I came home against his orders. I — I see what you're driving at! You're thinking of that dynamiting in Crowfoot Gulch. Oh, Matt, there was such a ghastly misunderstanding about that! After Dad drove you off our place, I demanded that he explain his rudeness. And he told me the truth of it."

"I'm listenin'," the Kid said woodenly.

"Dad was in Caprock that night, and he happened to see a bunch of riders head out of town leading a pack-horse with a box of dynamite on it. He thought Curly Bottsinger was heading the outfit, but he wasn't sure. Yet the more he thought about it, the more he wondered what Bottsinger intended doing with dynamite along the railroad right of way."

"He knew Bottsinger hated the railroad?"

She nodded. "He knew all right. Bottsinger hated Montana-Pacific because it meant the finish of his freight line. Dad hated the railroad, too. Oh, I'm not denying it! But Dad couldn't stomach underhanded fighting. He fretted about what was going on until he decided to follow those riders. He managed to trail them to Crowfoot Gulch. He left his horse behind and crept to a ledge for a better look, but he got there too late. He just barely had time to shelter himself behind an outcropping of rock when the blast went off."

"I savvy," said the Kid, but the skepticism in his voice gave his words the lie.

"But you don't!" she countered. "When you brought me back to the ranch, Dad recognized you as the man who'd jumped him in the gulch. All he could do that night was fight back. Don't you see? He made the same mistake you did. He thought *you* were one of the dynamiters. Do you wonder that he flew into a rage when he saw you again?"

Her lips quivered, but she mustered more words. "I'll always remember what you said when I thanked you for stopping the train and saving our lives," she went on.

"Have you forgotten? 'I just happened to be along,' you said. 'It might have been anybody.' In a way, Dad just happened to be along, too. Doesn't that entitle him to the benefit of the doubt, Matt?"

"It does," the Kid conceded. "And yet the whole thing is pat — too pat. He claims to be Tyler Whitman's friend in spite of their difference of opinion about the railroad. Why didn't your father tell Whitman about the explosion afterwards, instead of keeping quiet?"

"What was there to tell?" she countered wearily. "He couldn't even be positive it was Bottsinger he'd seen. And, besides, you don't understand Dad's viewpoint, Matt. He says he hates the railroad. The thing he really hates is what the coming of the railroad will mean. I hated it too, until you changed my mind by pointing out that what the railroad was doing to Caprock and Lazura was only temporary — that real towns would grow out of the dirt and debris of the hellish boomtowns.

"Maybe Dad will see it that way some day. Deep in his heart he has a real admiration for Tyler Whitman. I know it! And you can't overlook the fact that he delivered beef to Whitman, just as he promised he'd do. Only last week he told me he'd deliver more if Whitman's price was right. Our whole crew is back in the hills now, cutting out stuff to build another herd for the railroad."

"Why not?" the Kid rasped. "The rustling of railroad beef is finished now that Hidden Valley is no longer a secret. A man couldn't *pretend* to be selling beef to the railroad any longer. He couldn't make believe he was hazing steers toward the end o' steel when he'd know darn well they were going into a hole in the hills. He'd either have to actually deliver, or refuse to sell at all and admit he'd just as soon the graders went hungry. See how it adds up?"

While he'd spoken, his words tramping angrily on each other's heels, Tara had gone white. Now her eyes widened with horror. "I see . . ." she said, aghast. "I see it all! You think he's a — a Judas! You think he's one of the three men you're seeking!"

"God knows, I don't want to think it!"

the Kid countered, the anger gone out of him and his voice dull with pain. "I don't know, Tara . . . I don't know. But I've got to talk to him — straighten this thing out."

"No!" she cried, and swung her horse to block the trail. "I can't let you do that! Can't you understand? He cussed you because he thought you were a sneaking, underhanded dynamiter. He knows differently now, and he's sorry for that. But you're still a railroad man. Dad would be bitter and angry if you questioned him. His stiff-backed pride wouldn't let him be any other way. You're bitter too. If you accused him of being one of The Three, he might say he was, just to spite you and Tyler Whitman. What then, Matt?"

"No two men, born of the same woman, was ever so different as me and Hank," said the Kid, and wasn't conscious that he'd used those same words before. "But he was my brother. The blood call is a strong call, Tara. You know it too. That's why you're defending your father."

"Dad clings to an idea like a burr clings to a saddle-blanket," she said desperately. "He has the same opinion of you that I once had — the opinion we formed when we saw how Hank suffered for your sins. That's another reason I can't let you go to

Dad. He doesn't know that the Gospel Kid is a different man from Matt McGrath of Texas. He liked Hank a lot, Matt. If you knew how much, you'd know that Dad couldn't possibly be one of The Three."

But still the Kid's eyes were stern and unrelenting. They were very close to each other now, man and girl, and she laid a hand upon his shoulder as she lifted her eyes to his in a last appeal.

"Matt," she said, "every girl meets a certain man sometime — the *one* man. I always felt that I'd know mine the moment I first saw him. Would it make a difference to you if I told you I met him beyond Crowfoot Gulch? Would it matter if I told you I wanted to hate him when I discovered who he was — but that I couldn't?"

He gently took her hand from his shoulder. "Would it matter?" he repeated solemnly. "Let me tell you — I've been a tumbleweed, Tara; and I never cared much if I ever took root. Yet when I saw yonder Hidden Valley, I began figgerin' what a nice place it would be to have a spread with a few cattle under my iron. I've been dreamin' about such a place ever since — since the night I stopped the train. Don't you savvy how it is with me, Tara? Can't you understand that I've been fighting against a showdown with Storm Herndon — fighting for two months now?"

In that queer manner they declared their love for each other. And there was irony to transcend irony, because the thing that shone in her eyes was mirrored in the Kid's, and yet he couldn't consummate their declaration with a kiss, for there was still a lingering doubt in him.

"I want to believe you," he said hoarsely. "I — I do believe you. But why didn't you come and tell me the real reason why he ran me off his place? Two months I've waited and wondered . . ."

"I wanted to come," she said. "But I couldn't leave him again. You see, there's more to the story. When he rolled down the slope of the gulch that night, he landed in a cluster of rocks. He was hurt, but he managed to reach his horse and get away. Since then he's grown steadily worse. The doctor from Deadman says he'll get over it in a matter of time. But for the last two months he's scarcely been able to leave a chair. There is no bitterness like the bitterness of a cripple, Matt."

"*A cripple!*" the Kid echoed, horror in his voice, and then he was remembering Storm Herndon half rising from his chair on the ranch-house gallery only to settle back again. But the Kid was thinking of something else too, something that left him weak and trembling — a picture of himself forcing a showdown upon the fiery, vitriolic rancher — a picture of Storm Herndon going for his gun and he, the Kid, beating him to the draw, only to discover afterwards that the odds had all been in his favor because he'd fought a cripple.

"God!" he breathed.

"That's why I was repping for Dad with the herd," she went on. "I meant to tell you about it as we rode back to the ranch that day, but I knew you'd see for yourself when you met him."

"I'm sorry," he said humbly. "I'm mighty sorry, Tara. I never fought a man who wasn't able to fight back. Believe me. I —"

That was as far as he got. For suddenly guns were barking in the distance, echoing flatly along the coulee. Those guns were speaking at the H-in-a-Hat ranch-house, that deserted ranch-house where a crippled oldster waited, alone and defenseless. There was something ominous in the bark of those sixes, something that chilled the Kid. Tara lifted startled, fear-stricken eyes to his, and then he and the girl were spurring their horses, single-filing in a wild gallop down the coulee which broadened

240

out where the ranch buildings sprawled ahead of them.

Thundering away in the opposite direction, their bodies bent low over saddle-horns, were seven riders. Leading them was Cisco Yawberry, a bearded giant in a saddle. There was no mistaking him. His gun leaping into his hand, the Kid sprayed lead after them. But the distance was already too great, and he let them go, following Tara who was hurling herself from her horse and running toward the long gallery.

Then the Kid saw what had caught Tara's eye and was drawing her upon flying feet. And the sight was proof enough that Storm Herndon was no ally of The Three. Cisco Yawberry rode for that ruthless trio, and Yawberry had come there to kill. No mistake about that, either. Storm Herndon lay upon the planking of the gallery in a shapeless heap, his face gray, his shirt-front soggy with blood.

17.

The man and the girl looked at each other across the body of the unconscious rancher, after the Kid had made a brief examination of the wound.

"He's alive," said the Kid. He was always to remember that she said nothing then, or ever, to remind him that he had misjudged Storm Herndon.

"How badly is he hurt?" she asked, and drew a look of admiration from the Kid because her voice was so firm.

The Kid didn't lie. Along his smoky back-trail he'd seen many men laid low by lead, and he could gauge the seriousness of Herndon's wound with an accuracy that was almost professional.

"He's got to get to a doctor — as fast as we can get him there," he said. "I've fished out a few bullets in my time, but I wouldn't dare probe for that one. It's too near his heart. Can you get a wagon ready?"

By the time she had a team hitched to a wagon, he'd rummaged inside the house and found bandages and whiskey for an antiseptic, and had doctored the stricken rancher as best he could. Herndon's pulse was feeble, but the thread of life was there. The two of them lifted him into the wagon bed with infinite care, making the unconscious man as comfortable as possible in a nest of blankets.

Inside the house, the Kid had noticed a rifle laid across a set of deer horns which were nailed above the doorway. He fetched the rifle along, laying it in the wagon bed. The girl saw him do it, but it wasn't until they'd put the ranch-house behind them that she spoke.

"Do you think Yawberry and those others will be back?" she asked.

The Kid nodded. "When we come chargin' down the coulee, they probably figgered the whole H-in-a-Hat crew was burning leather," he reflected. "Also, Yawberry must have thought that your dad was dead. If that bunch is still hangin' around close enough to see us packin' him off, they'll figger what's up. We've got to keep an eye peeled."

He threw a glance over his shoulder.

"They must have learned that Dad was going to keep on supplying M.P. with beef," Tara said. "Yawberry was sent here to kill him if there was no other way of stopping him, it seems. Dad's death would intimidate the other Deadman ranchers, make them think twice about bucking The Three."

"He isn't dead," the Kid reminded her. "The doc out at end of steel is a mighty good medico, a sawbones who could be making a big name for himself back East. He'll patch up your dad pronto."

After that there were few words between them. The Kid was busy with the reins, and Tara, more often than not, was back in the wagon bed, crouching beside the still figure of her father. The Kid's eyes were to the rear as often as they were to the front. The ranch buildings were out of sight, for they'd climbed from the coulee that cupped them. The prairie lay naked and serene, peaceful as paradise and just about as pretty.

But there was a deceptiveness to the calm, and when the horsemen appeared — seven of them — debouching from the coulee to pour across the plain behind them, the Kid was in no ways astonished.

"They're coming," he said evenly.

And coming they were, shooting as they roared in pursuit. They were too far behind to use their six-guns effectively, and it was a gesture born of instinct rather than reason that sent the Kid's hand to his hip to scatter lead in return. He'd been holding the wagon to a crawling pace across the rough terrain, mindful of the misery of the man who was bedded down among the blankets. He still held the wagon at that same pace, though Yawberry's bunch, galloping hard, was rapidly eating up the distance between them.

"The whip!" Tara frantically cried from the back of the wagon. "Go ahead and use the whip, Matt! We've got to outrun them!"

"You figger — ?" the Kid began to shout, but he'd already guessed her thought. Tara was reasoning that no harm that haste could do to Storm Herndon would be as great as the harm he'd suffer if Yawberry's crew overtook them. To race the team was to gamble with death, but if the team were held in check there wouldn't even be a gambling chance for any of them. So the Kid plied the whip, laying it along the backs of the team. Jolting and careening, the wagon bounced across the prairie as the horses stretched against their harness.

Yet the outcome of the race was bound to be disaster for the Kid and the Herndons. The team, hauling the heavy wagon, couldn't hope to outpace the fleet-footed saddlers behind. Each glance told the Kid that the pursuers were gaining. Before a mile had unreeled, the Kid knew it was going to take lead to match lead.

"Tara!" he called. "Take the reins!"

She obediently climbed up into the lurching seat and took the ribbons from him. Freed, the Kid tumbled back into the wagon bed, clawing desperately for the rifle. Yawberry's bunch weren't many hundred yards behind now. Cradling the rifle against his cheek, the Kid hauled away on the trigger, firing again and again. And before that first barrage, one rustler flung his hands toward the sky and pitched from his saddle to the ground, where he lay in a sprawling heap.

The Kid shouted in triumph. They were still coming, but some of their self-confidence was gone. They were spreading out now, fanning wide instead of holding together as a compact bunch. The Kid scattered more lead, and saw another rustler clasp his side, then frantically clutch his saddle-horn with both hands as he reeled and teetered.

Considering that the wagon was leaping and lurching like some live thing, it was mighty good shooting, the Kid decided, and gave himself a mental pat on the back. But it wasn't his marksmanship alone that was spreading consternation among the ranks of Yawberry's men. He had them outranged. With the rifle he could keep them at a distance so great that their own six-guns were ineffective weapons. It was all aces for the Kid, and he played them systematically.

But suddenly this running fight was over. He saw Yawberry jerk up his hand for attention. The giant shouted something to his men, but the words were lost in the distance. Then they were all angling toward the west, bee-lining across the prairie and away, putting their backs to the wagon they'd been trying to overtake.

The Kid frowned, signalling to Tara to ease up on the whip. Dropping the hot rifle, he climbed back to the seat, taking the reins from her. "They've had a belly-full, looks like," he commented.

"But they'll be back," she said. "They probably intend to circle ahead and waylay us somewhere."

"Not much chance of that, on this flat prairie," he argued. "No, I've got a feeling that they've given up for good. But still it doesn't make sense. It's almost like they'd spent as much time as they dared, trying to run us down, and now they've got something more *important* to do. Glad as I am to be rid of them, I don't like the smell of this!"

Silence fell between them then, and even though the menace of Yawberry's bunch had dissolved in the remote distance, it was a nightmare journey, an endless trek along an endless trail. And once the aftermath of excitement had left the Kid, contrition rode with him that weary day. For with him, always, was the remembrance that he had passed judgment on an innocent man. Coupled with his regret was a determination to save the life of Storm Herndon if human endeavor could make that miracle possible.

He wondered whether it might have been best to have ridden after the doctor and fetched the medico to the H-in-a-Hat. But that would have necessitated covering twice as many miles, even though he could travel a great deal faster in a saddle than upon this wagon seat. Also, it would have meant leaving Tara and her father alone at the ranch-house while he made the trip. Scant chance the two of them would have stood against another attack by Yawberry!

Yet even now the Kid's urge was to lash the team into a gallop, but upon rough ground he didn't dare. He had to crawl along, seemingly at a snail's pace, conscious that the slightest jar might lessen Herndon's chance of living. There was no way of gauging the amount of harm that had been done to the man by that wild ride to outrun Yawberry's bunch. But Storm Herndon was still alive, for once he opened his eyes.

"You ain't tellin' me who I can sell my beef to!" he muttered feverishly, then lapsed into unconsciousness again.

Obviously he was deliriously repeating something he'd said to Cisco Yawberry when that rustler and his crew had swooped down upon the ranch — evidence enough that Tara's theory regarding the shooting was correct. The Kid's eyes were constantly peeled for Yawberry as they rolled along. But the rustlers had long since vanished and the prairie still lay naked before them. The long day spent itself at last and darkness overtook them, but still they plodded onward.

Now the Kid was more alert than ever, for if Yawberry planned to waylay them somewhere up ahead, the night would give the rustlers an advantage. But at least there'd be a moon to minimize that advantage and to light the way. The Kid, guided by Tara, who knew that range, came upon a road of sorts, so the wounded man was not jostled so badly as he'd been. With the moon climbing above them, and the stars sparkling against the velvet canopy of the heavens, they headed southward, always southward. And sometime during the night they finally reached the rails.

Eastward to Deadman town now, or westward to end o' steel? The Kid wasted no time making a decision. "End o' steel is closer, and chances are the sawbones will be there," he said. "If he isn't, we can always pack your dad back to town by train."

She smiled wanly at such an idea. "We'll have to keep him unconscious if we expect to get *him* on a train, I imagine," she said. "And we'll probably have to hog-tie him as well!"

The Kid turned the team to the west and paralleled the rails. He watched for the beam of a locomotive's head lamp now, hoping that a work train might be coming out of Deadman, bringing an off-shift crew back to the construction camp. If a train came along, he could flag it down and get Storm Herndon into camp far faster than this slow-moving wagon was taking him. But the moon had faded by the time they reached the railroad tunnel, and with it had faded the Kid's hope that a train might be running that night.

He'd been through M.P.'s tunnel too many times not to know that there wasn't room enough for a wagon to skirt the tracks inside the bore. He had to force the team up onto the tracks then, a process that shook the wagon violently. Tara cradled her father's head in her lap, easing some of the shock. Then they were into the black depth of the tunnel, guided only by the rails they followed. As fervently as the Kid had prayed for the coming of a train before, he now prayed that the track would be clear. They reached the western end of the tunnel safely and the Kid sighed his relief.

"Four — five miles to camp," he told the girl.

Dawn was breaking behind them as they came to the end of steel. It had taken the Kid almost twice as long to make the return journey as it had taken him to ride to the H-in-a-Hat from this same camp. But at least the flame of life still flickered in the breast of Storm Herndon, and the gruelling race with death was nearly won.

Or so the Kid thought. That was before they rounded a curve to see the camp sprawled ahead, for the Kid knew instantly that something was almighty wrong here.

Men were swarming everywhere, pouring from tents and construction shacks in various stages of undress, rushing about for all the world like a leaderless drove of ants. Someone pounded an iron triangle. On a siding a locomotive puffed, its whistle beginning to scream as the Kid looked upon the wild confusion in amazement.

Tyler Whitman was in the midst of it all, bareheaded, his gray hair flying as he gesticulated with his arms, issuing orders that were lost in the roar of startled voices. Leaping from the wagon seat, the Kid stumbled stiffly to him.

"What's going on?" he demanded.

"You're back, Matt!" Whitman roared. "Good! We'll need you. It's a showdown, that's what it is! Central Western has struck — and struck hard. Damn it all, man, I should have expected something like this! We've got them licked, so they've become desperate. They're risking everything to break our backs with one blow!"

"But where?" the Kid asked. "Just where are they striking?"

"In Deadman. All night long Bottsinger's stage coaches and freight wagons have been bringing men into town —

toughs from the Central Western camps. They're taking over Deadman town — lock, stock and barrel. Don't you see what it means? They can tear up our tracks if necessary, keep supplies from coming through to us from the East, disrupt our communication system. Without steel we're bogged down — licked!"

"Storm Herndon's in yonder wagon," the Kid reported hastily, with a jerk of his thumb. "He was shot down, wounded bad, because he insisted on selling beef to you. Where's the doc?"

"Storm — wounded!" Whitman said dazedly, and groaned. "The doctor went into Deadman with Kurt Ormond before the trouble broke. Key O'Dade started a message through when the toughs began taking over the town. Either the wire was cut, or Key was dragged away from the instrument. The line's dead."

"And the doc's in town!" the Kid said, and saw a hope die.

"But wait!" Whitman interjected. "I'm taking every man into Deadman to give them their fight. I'll hook on my own coach too. Get some boys and have Storm loaded into it. We'll get him to the doctor!"

"Mister, I'm working for the railroad

again," the Kid shouted, and was off.

If there had been confusion before, it was thrice multiplied as a locomotive backed up to a string of flatcars with Tyler Whitman's private coach coupled to the front of them. Onto the flatcars piled the workers of M.P., hundreds of them, and even horses, used by the grading crews, were forced up plank inclines to be taken along.

There were very few guns in the camp, but those that were available were passed around. The rest of the men chose hickory pickhandles for their weapons, or any other sort of club they could lay their hands on.

Tyler Whitman personally supervised the loading of Storm Herndon into his own car behind the locomotive and climbed in after the rancher. The Kid had one last glimpse of the pale, strained face of Tara as she followed her father. Then the Kid swung into the locomotive cab just as the huge iron monster lurched to life, slowly gathering momentum as it rolled along the unballasted roadway.

They were on their way to Deadman — the whole fighting force of the Montana-Pacific. They were on their way to meet the challenge of Central Western. But the Kid couldn't help but wonder if they were too late to prevent the vandalism that would spell the finish of M.P.

It was a desperate play the rival railroad was making, but it might work for them. If Central Western was victorious today, then Central Western would be victorious in the race for government subsidization. Let the matter come to court later, C.W. would argue. How could a bankrupt Montana-Pacific wage a courtroom battle?

No, the real fight would be in Deadman. There was Shadow Loomis to be considered, but even though Loomis might report his findings to his superiors later, tell the truth about Central Western's lawless methods, Loomis would be only one small voice. And Shadow Loomis, the Kid remembered, might not even be alive to speak his piece, for the man had already been warned by The Three.

The Kid's head was craned from the cab window while a sweating fireman toiled beside him. They were almost to the tunnel, and because the Kid had been thinking of Shadow Loomis, his astonishment was the greater when he found himself seeing Loomis!

The man was ahead of them, in the middle of the track. He had suddenly disgorged from the tunnel's black mouth, astride a horse, and he was racing down the track, straight toward the oncoming train. Gesticulating wildly, he was trying to flag down the train just as the Kid had once done.

The engineer, leaning from the opposite window, saw the government man at the same time, and reached for the brake lever. Steel ground against steel as the train slid to a stop. The Kid was out of the cab just as Loomis flung himself from his horse.

"Thank God you stopped in time!" the government man panted. "You can't go through that tunnel. It's doomed!"

"Doomed!" the Kid echoed. "You mean — ?"

"It's going to be dynamited! Remember I told you that I was going to take to the hills for a while? Not more than half an hour ago, I saw riders working with dynamite, tamping charges into drill holes above the eastern end of the tunnel. The head of the outfit was that bearded fellow who's been around Deadman a time or two — Yawberry, I think they call him. They're going to close the tunnel, I tell you!"

So shooting Storm Herndon wasn't the only devil's work that Cisco Yawberry was supposed to do for The Three! Now the Kid knew why Yawberry had given up the chase out there on the prairie and angled to the west. But that wasn't what made the Kid stare, horror and despair in his eyes.

The tunnel was doomed! A thousand tons of rock and earth would soon be blocking it, making it impassable for weeks. Truly, The Three had planned a master stroke to defeat M.P., for the fighting forces of Montana-Pacific would be shut off from Deadman. They might reach the town by other routes, afoot and on horseback, but they'd be too late. And Storm Herndon, who was dying in Whitman's coach, would never get to the doctor in time.

"How soon will they be lighting the fuse?" the Kid demanded, his fingers digging into Loomis' arm. "Tell me quick! How much time is there left?"

"I don't know," Loomis said shakily. "My idea was to get away and stop any train that might be coming through. Maybe there's plenty of time left. Or maybe the fuse has already been fired. *Man, you aren't thinking of — ?*"

But the Kid was swinging back into the cab. "I could pass the word back along the flatcars and take a vote on whether we should take the chance," he said swiftly. "That would take time — time we haven't got to spare. I know these M.P. men, Loomis. I've worked with them for weeks, and I'm thinkin' I know the way they'd want to do this. Engineer, are you a gamblin' man — or have I gotta try my hand at runnin' this iron cayuse myself? *We're going through that tunnel!*"

The engineer nodded, tight-lipped. "If this train is going any place, I'm going with it," he said, and tugged at the throttle.

Shadow Loomis, something of both admiration and awe in his face, swung into the cab. Right behind him came Tyler Whitman, who'd clambered from his own coach to learn the cause of the stop.

The Kid explained quickly. ". . . I had to make the decision for you," he concluded.

"But Herndon's girl!" Whitman exclaimed. "She's aboard too!"

He didn't need to remind the Kid. But Matt McGrath had thought of many things in this last minute — the brave tilt of Tara's chin as she'd asked how badly her father was wounded — her shouted, "Go ahead and use the whip, Matt!" — her stoical suffering on the long ride across the prairie. The life of Storm Herndon depended on his getting into Deadman regardless of consequences, just as it had depended upon outrunning Cisco Yawberry. The Kid had made Tara's decision for her, knowing full well what her own decision would have been.

"She'd want it this way, Whitman," he said softly.

And now the drivers had spun and caught, and the train was moving forward, picking up speed as it went. The dark mouth of the tunnel yawned before them. They were swallowed by it, and only the glow of the firebox broke the enveloping darkness. A hush fell upon the five men who shared the cab, and the same thought might have been in the mind of each:

How many seconds until the mountain came down on top of them?

18.

To the Kid it seemed as though the train
crept at a snail's pace through the tunnel,
but that was only because time was standing
still. Actually the locomotive had gathered
speed, and in spite of the drag of the heavy
load behind, it was running the tunnel far
faster than it had ever been run before. The
engineer, his face ghastly and sweat-
streaked, was well aware that he was racing
with doom.

His head poked out of the cab window,
the Kid saw the white eye of the tunnel's
end through the choking, blinding smoke
that bannered backward into his face. The
Kid ceased to breathe. How far away that
daylight seemed!

Every sound was magnified in that man-
made cavern — the scream of steam from
the pistons, the pound of drivers over the
unleveled rails, even the scrape of the fireman's shovel as he heaved coal into the
firebox in a frenzy of effort. Yet above all
that bedlam, the Kid's ears were alert for
the crack of doom, the first faint sound

that might herald a devastating blast.

He heard it, too. But not until the locomotive had hurtled into the feeble dawn light again — and not until the last human, freighted flatcar was in the clear.

Then the explosion came, the roar of it shaking the locomotive. Before the Kid's horrified eyes as he gazed to the rear, the face of the mountain writhed, and the walls above the tunnel groaned and collapsed. Then there was only billowing dust, the roar of a dynamite-sired avalanche, and the tunnel was sealed behind them.

"Stop the train!" Tyler Whitman ordered grimly, and the Kid wondered if his own face was as white and strained as the railroad builder's. When the locomotive squealed to a stop again, Whitman piled out of the cab and away. He returned very shortly.

"Get going!" he said briefly to the engineer, then turned to the Kid. "I unloaded a dozen men with guns and horses," Whitman explained. "Picked men. Those dynamiters aren't far away, and my boys have orders to round them up if it takes until doomsday. The rest of us will clean up Deadman. We can still do that, at least."

After that he had little to say. The locomotive was moving again, and this time the heart of the iron cayuse might have really been in the race. With flanges screaming as they struck curve after curve, the cab swaying and pitching, it roared down the track toward Deadman, the engineer throwing his weight upon the whistle cord while the Kid spelled the weary fireman.

Matt McGrath was working for the railroad again. And in this, Montana-Pacific's darkest hour, he sensed just how much the road had come to mean to him.

Yes, Montana-Pacific had a personal significance in the Kid's scheme of things now. Once he'd wanted to see the road finished because it had been Hellvation Hank's dream. Once he'd served the road because its enemies were his enemies — The Three. But in the crucible of sweat and strife, through the long days when toil and danger had marked the inching of the steel toward the sunset, there'd been a change in Matt McGrath. At heart he was still a son of the saddle. When the railroad was finished, his day with it would be finished. But until that day came, the fight of Montana-Pacific would be his fight and his heart would be in it.

"I'm glad I got back in time," he told

Tyler Whitman as Shadow Loomis took the shovel. "I'll be in on the big battle, at any rate."

"Every fighting man will count, son," Whitman said. "I'm mighty glad you finished your other business and came back to us, too."

The Kid told him about it then, told him of the suspicion that had grown within him concerning Storm Herndon; and of the way that suspicion had been proved unfounded. Whitman heard him out in stupefied silence.

"If only you'd told me this in the first place!" the railroad builder said. "You see, I know Storm Herndon — better, perhaps, than he knows himself. He'd fight my road, yes. But he wouldn't fight me personally, no more than he would have fought Hank. Shooting down Hank or dynamiting one of my trestles just wouldn't be in Storm's line. We were his friends — Hank especially."

"I knew that," said the Kid. "But —"

"Storm Herndon was closer to Hank than anybody," Whitman went on. "When we planned to send Hank's Bible to you, and couldn't be sure of your whereabouts, I told Kurt Ormond to check up with Storm Herndon before he got the package off to you. I figured that if Hank had mentioned your address to any man, it was likely to have been to old Storm and —"

"Wait!" the Kid interjected, his eyes shining with a growing thought. "Are you saying that Kurt Ormond had Hank's Bible — that he was the one who sent it to me?"

"I wrote the letter that went with it," Whitman explained. "I did that the day of Hank's funeral. I stayed for the service, but I was overdue back at division headquarters and had to leave Caprock. Kurt checked on your address and handled the details for me."

"I see," the Kid said slowly. "That explains why Kurt knew so much about me and —"

His speech broke in the middle, for Deadman was sprawling before them. The locomotive was wheezing to a stop, its fighting freight unloading to swarm forward, eager to get into the coming fray.

Up ahead the narrow street was clogged with men — the Central Western toughs who'd been brought in overnight by The Three to take over the town and thereby throttle the Montana-Pacific. They were pouring toward the tracks, those toughs, a surly, shouting mob, and the M.P. men met the challenge of that oncoming fury by charging to meet them. A wild cry welled above the pounding of boots as the two factions crashed together. With no more prelude than that, the battle was under way.

It was only by an effort that the Kid managed to restrain six of the M.P. men, and to these he gave special orders that sent them hurrying away in six different directions. Afterwards the Kid climbed into Whitman's private coach where Storm Herndon lay silent and gray-faced, but still breathing. Tara hovered near him.

"Six men have gone to look for the sawbones," the Kid explained to the girl. "They all know him by sight, and he shouldn't be hard to find. There's no reason why those toughs should have molested the doc, and he'll likely be here pronto. He can work on your dad right here in this car."

He moved toward the door, but Tara caught his arm. "And you, Matt?" she asked.

"I'll keep an eye peeled for the doc, too," he promised. "But the men will find him, I know. Me, I've got somebody else to look for, too. The Three are here in Deadman, Tara."

"Once I wanted you to leave them be," she said. "But I've seen too much of their devilish work since then. Just be careful, Matt! For my sake, be careful."

He kissed her then, holding her close for an endless moment. It was their first kiss, and the thought that shadowed the Kid was that it might be their last and have to do for all eternity. This was August the second, wasn't it? The day The Three had decreed he should die. Reluctantly he pulled himself away, swinging out of the car without a word.

Chaos ruled the street stretching ahead of him, a savage confusion of fighting men milling to make a sea of waving pick-handles. Guns popped here and there, the sound of them almost lost in the roar of cursing voices. The Kid shouldered into the thick of it ruthlessly, his left fist lashing out, his right arm arcing as he laid his gun-barrel across head after head, seeing men drop before him, seeing others push forward to take their places.

He caught a glimpse of Tyler Whitman, gray hair flying, and saw that soldierly old-ster fighting hand to hand with a burly tough. And he saw Shadow Loomis, the man who'd been sent there to be a non-partisan observer, lay that same tough low as the fellow pressed Whitman too hard.

It was tooth and toenail — fist and club and gun and boot. It was hell unleashed, men slugging and wrestling along the entire length of the street, crowding against the buildings and churning the dust between them.

Yet the Montana-Pacific men were fighting with the greatest fury, throwing their hearts and souls as well as their battered bodies into the conflict, fighting as though this had become a personal affair — which indeed it had. The Montana-Pacific men were remembering that dynamited tunnel, and the fate that would have been theirs if the blast had gone off a minute or two sooner. Montana-Pacific was out for vengeance.

A club caught the Kid along the side of his head. He escaped the full force of the blow, for he saw it coming and twisted aside. But he lost his footing and went down, his head ringing, and was swept beneath a wave of flashing legs and trampling boots. He managed to get to his feet again and saw the red thatch of Key O'Dade in the press of men ahead of him. The Kid thrilled to the sight. He'd feared that the telegrapher might have paid with his life for trying to get a message through to warn the end o' steel camp of the raid.

But O'Dade was there, fighting as savagely as any of the others, throwing himself into the conflict with a Celt's natural aptitude for such work.

There were other faces the Kid recognized, too, the faces of men with whom he'd worked through all the weary days when the steel had pushed from Caprock to Lazura and Deadman and beyond. But the Kid searched the most intently for the faces of the foe, yet nowhere did he see Hoyt Durham or Curly Bottsinger or the third man he sought.

That was why he squeezed through the writhing wall of bodies and into the doorway of the Golden Slipper as quickly as he could. The saloon was Durham's stronghold, and it was the logical place to look for the man, since Durham obviously wasn't in the fighting out on the street. Inside the Golden Slipper, the Kid sagged against the wall, panting and waiting for his head to clear completely. Standing there, his clothes torn and disheveled, his chest heaving, he was amazed to find the place absolutely deserted.

He hadn't been in the Golden Slipper since it had moved to Deadman, for Whitman's decree had barred all M.P. men from the place. Besides, the Kid had kept away from Hoyt Durham during the period when the Kid had suspected Storm Herndon of being one of The Three. He'd heard that Durham's business had suffered greatly because of Whitman's blacklisting of the saloon. Most of the percentage girls, according to rumor, had deserted the Golden Slipper for more lucrative pleasure places. But the Kid had hardly expected to find the Golden Slipper completely empty.

Yet it was. The shelves were only half stocked with liquor, and there were plenty of empty bottles about, proof that the Central Western toughs had roistered there the night before, fortifying themselves with liquor before they went about the devil's work they'd come to do. But the place was silent and empty, its silence accentuated by the roar of the street fighting, the sound of the tumult beating through the thin walls. The Kid crossed toward the bar, his boot heels thundering in the shrouding hush of the room.

That was when he felt unseen eyes watching him. He spun about, gun in hand, his own eyes probing every shadowy corner. For suddenly the feeling was strong upon him that he was in greater danger there than he'd been in the street where death ran rampant and disaster had a hundred forms. He tried to shake that feeling away, but it persisted. Yet where was the danger in that deserted place?

He approached the bar, wondering if he'd find a barkeep cowering behind the long counter. His eyes flicked to the full-length mirror behind the bar. As on that other time when he'd walked into the Golden Slipper in Caprock, he saw the reflections of the oil paintings on the wall behind him, especially the one called "The Lady of the Nile." And, unbelievably, just for a second the picture had the semblance of life once again, just as it had had that other time.

But this time the Kid understood — and realized his own danger in the same moment!

Shadow Loomis had been in Hoyt Durham's office once, had, according to his own admission, searched the place. Shadow Loomis knew the secret of that trick picture. Loomis had even spoken of it to the Kid, warning the trouble-shooter in a way, that day they'd first met in Caprock. The Kid had failed to understand at the time.

"A pretty picture, eh?" the man had said.

". . . She can see, friend; and she can hear. And some day she'll speak. You mark my word and don't forget it . . ."

It had sounded idiotic at the time, like the mouthings of a madman. How could a picture speak? But "The Lady of the Nile" was speaking now, speaking with a fiery tongue that blazed from her face. Gun-flame was lashing through the picture — spearing straight at the Kid!

He felt the burn of the bullet as it bored into his thigh, spinning him violently about and slamming him hard against the bar. His knees caved and he fell to the floor, fighting against the crowding darkness that threatened to claim him. Lying there like a dead man, his pain-fogged thought was that such was the way of The Three, to strike from cover, to shoot a man down without warning just as they'd shot Hell-vation Hank.

Something in that thought gave the Kid the strength to clutch the edge of the bar and pull himself to his feet. "The Lady of the Nile" still smiled down upon him, but her beauty was marred beyond repair, for there was a bullet hole where her mouth should have been. The Kid wondered if she would speak again, or if by falling he'd fooled the hidden assassin who lurked behind the painting into thinking he was dead.

There had to be a room somewhere up above, a room behind that picture, a room where The Three would be hiding. The Kid could see stairs in one shadowy corner, flimsy stairs leading to the second floor. Very slowly he tottered toward those steps, wondering the while if his strength would sustain him until he reached them.

19.

Hoyt Durham's private office in Deadman's Golden Slipper was much as his offices in Lazura and Caprock had been — another ornately furnished room built below the floor level of the second story, with steps leading down into it from a regular second floor door.

In this, the latest of his windowless sanctuaries, Durham came to his feet, letting the leather flap on the wall fall into place. He blew the smoke from the barrel of his gun before sliding the weapon into a shoulder holster.

"Got him!" he announced, his swarthy face triumphant in the glow of the lamp upon the centering table. "That idea you once had of shooting through the picture made it a cinch, Curly. Lucky we heard him walking around down there. He'll do no more walking. Matt McGrath is stretched out on the floor — dead!"

Curly Bottsinger grinned, stepped across the room and had a look for himself. Seated again, he glanced at his misshapen knuckles. "Reckon that's news enough to make it a good day," he said. "Maybe we'd better tote his carcass out of the place, though."

The third man, seated in a shadowy corner, shook his head.

"No hurry," he argued. "And we won't have to pack him far. There'll be plenty of dead men in this town before the sun goes down. And there'll be nobody to ask questions about them. Tyler Whitman will be broke, and his backers will have had a bellyfull of financing him. Montana-Pacific Railroad will gather rust. We'll be the winners, gentlemen, and the winners don't have to answer to anybody."

"Just the same, things could 'a' broke better for us," Bottsinger, always the pessimist, complained. "Yawberry shore never blew that tunnel shut in time or M.P. wouldn't have got a train into town. And we'd have stopped that train if we'd put the toughs to work tearing up track last night, instead of swillin' free liquor downstairs. And what about this Loomis galoot? You had a hunch he was a professional snoop of some kind. Supposing he's snooping for the government, like you figgered he might be? Supposing he reports this raid and Central Western has to answer for it?"

The third man eased his gun from its holster, spun the cylinder thoughtfully and replaced the weapon.

"We gave Loomis until the fifteenth to run or take the consequences," he reflected. "But we won't wait that long. No use leaving any loose ends. I didn't see Loomis around last night, but he's probably still in town. Who's to say what happened if he stops a bullet during the street fighting? If there's a government investigation on account of him, we'll claim M.P. started the fracas when we brought men into town for our own protection. We'll say Loomis got cut down during the fight. One of us had better get outside and find him."

"That'll be pretty risky," Durham observed. "From the sound of things, that street's no place for a man with any respect for his own hide. Let's cut for low card to see who does the job."

He bustled about the room in search of a deck of cards, finding one in a commodious drawer of his desk after a lengthy search. Breaking the seal, he shuffled the pasteboards, his jeweled fingers winking in the lamplight as he fanned out the cards, face down, on the table top. Each man selected a card for himself, the third man smiling as he faced his — the deuce of clubs.

"That's about the way it should be," Durham reflected. "We're starting around the circle again. I burned down Matt McGrath. Curly, here, got Dan Callishaw. And you're the gent who pumped a bullet into Hellvation Hank. Now it's your turn again. You —"

Curly Bottsinger had stepped toward the wall and crouched to have another look beneath the leather flap. It was his wild exclamation that silenced Durham.

"He's gone!" Bottsinger shouted. "McGrath! He ain't down below!"

"Reckon not," said the Gospel Kid. He'd opened the door and was standing framed in the doorway, a bloody, disheveled figure. But the gun in his hand was steady enough. "Raise 'em!" he ordered. "*Careful, Ormond!* You'll never get that gun out of leather!"

Thus Matt McGrath looked down upon The Three, the trio he'd trailed so long, watching as they slowly hoisted their hands — Hoyt Durham and Curly Bottsinger, and the third man, Kurt Ormond, construction engineer for the Montana-Pacific! Amazingly, Ormond, exposed at long last, was the coolest of the trio. He'd gestured toward his gun at the Kid's appearance, but now he stood with hands raised, smiling.

"So now you know," he said evenly.

"Now I know you're the one who shot down Hank," the Kid said. "I heard Durham put the deadwood on you just as I stood outside the door, a second before Bottsinger took a look and found I wasn't downstairs. But I'm not surprised to find that you're one of The Three, Ormond. You see, you gave yourself away."

"I don't think so," Ormond scoffed. "The man who made a slip was Hoyt when he thought you were dead just because you fell after he shot you."

"You slipped too, Ormond. You slipped when you had that headboard left in my tent — with my birth date on it. That puzzled me for a spell. I couldn't figger how anybody hereabouts knew my birth date. Not until Whitman told me this morning that you had Hank's Bible for a while last fall. *My birth date was written in that Bible, on the family record page!* The same page where Hank had penciled the last address of mine he'd happened to have. You've got a good memory, Ormond. Or did you figger, even last fall, that knowing my birth date might come in handy sometime?"

Ormond laughed. "Since you were born on the first day of the year, January first was easy to remember. Somehow the year stuck in my mind, too. When we made up that headboard, I thought it would be more impressive with your birth date. I never guessed you'd be able to figure out where the information came from. For other gents we had Thackery Weaver's list. He was always bragging about how thorough his paper was, so we borrowed the data from his files."

"I know," said the Kid. "Was a time when I thought Weaver might be one of The Three. I know different now. You're Judas all right, Ormond — a sneaking double-crosser who pretended to work for the Montana-Pacific when the sign says you've been on Central Western's payroll all along. No wonder you didn't want that fellow hung off Crowfoot trestle. And I can savvy now why you tried to keep me from tackling Curly Bottsinger the day I caught him slowing down the track-layers. A heap of things are clear. You're a sight worse than the first Judas! He was decent enough to string himself up afterwards!"

"Judas?" Ormond repeated. "You mean — ?"

"I mean I've been looking for three gents — gents like Goliath and Herod and Judas. Hank must have known that one of the

278

three of you had burned him down. He managed to leave that much sign for me!"

Ormond's eyes widened, and for the first time he was visibly astonished. "Those blood smears in Hank's Bible!" he gasped. "I saw them too! But I thought Hank had probably pawed the pages accidentally as he lay dying . . ."

All this talk wasn't fooling the Kid. Ormond was stalling for time, postponing the inevitable reckoning. But within the Kid was a great weariness, and a desire to be done with this business.

"One of you is as guilty as another," he said with the solemnity of a judge pronouncing sentence. "There's Hellvation Hank to be accounted for, and Dan Callishaw, and Hanson, and a cowboy named Dave Woods, and others that was either killed by your hands or by your orders. It's been a long trail, and this is the end of it. But the hell of it is that I can't shoot you down . . ."

Bottsinger stared at him incredulously. "You mean you ain't gonna gun us?" he demanded.

"Not the way you think," the Kid said. "Not the way you'd do business — you back-shootin' skunks! Was a time when I wouldn't even be wastin' words on you.

They'd tell you that along the Rio. You can thank Hellvation Hank for the chance you're going to get."

"Chance?" Durham echoed. He'd seized upon the word avidly.

"I had to study Hank's Bible," the Kid went on, "to read the sign he'd left for me. And reading that Bible, I began to see that my way was the wrong way. That's what's made the difference between the Gospel Kid and Matt McGrath of Texas. But Hank was my brother, and I'm not forgettin' that, either. 'Vengeance is mine,' sayeth the Lord.' But maybe I'm to be His instrument of vengeance today. But — hell! You don't even savvy what I'm talkin' about!"

He slipped his gun into its holster. *"Get at it!"* he said with a vast disgust.

Just for an instant he stood there weaponless, giving them the fighting chance they hadn't given Hank McGrath or Dan Callishaw. Then, their first astonishment passing, they were doing exactly what the Kid had known they would do — going for their guns.

Hoyt Durham was the first to unlimber his six-shooter, and Durham was the first to die. The Kid's hand darted downward and came up with fire blossoming from it.

He shot Durham just as the dandified saloon-owner was earing back the hammer of his weapon.

But that split second had given Bottsinger and Ormond time to get their guns into action. Those guns spat simultaneously, driving splinters from the door jamb on either side of the Kid. Leaping down into the room, the Kid felt the burn of a bullet along his shoulder, the bite of another as it nicked the lobe of his ear. But he was firing before his feet touched the floor, and Bottsinger crumpled into a corner, a grotesque heap with a bullet hole between his shaggy brows.

The Kid landed sprawling, for the excruciating pain that welled from his wounded thigh as he struck the floor made his legs turn rubbery beneath him. A bullet zipped over his head as he went down, and another broke the skin over one of his ribs. Kurt Ormond was firing with the same phenomenal coolness that characterized his every move.

But the Kid was just as cool, and a great deal more methodical. Propping himself upon one elbow, he sighted carefully, taking an eternity to aim at the engineer, another eternity to squeeze the trigger. The gun belched and Ormond wilted before him.

"You — win . . ." Ormond managed to say, and for once the mask-like expression was gone from his inscrutable face, and there was something in his eyes that might have been awe. "Told you once — you were an all-around — fighting man," he gasped. "We should — have had you — on our side . . ." He pitched face-forward, dead.

It was over — but there was an aftermath. Ormond, in life, had been the brains of The Three and therefore the most formidable one of that deadly trio. Now that he was dead, it was as though his power for evil lived after him. For Ormond's fingers clawed at the table as he fell, fastening upon the silk tablecloth. As the cloth was wrenched away, the lamp overturned. Instantly burning kerosene was showering everywhere, lapping across the floor toward the flimsy walls as a sheet of flame reared itself across the room.

Out of that inferno the Kid dragged himself, managing to get to his feet in the door-studded hallway of the second floor. With the wall to support him, he groped toward the stairs, the smoke billowing down the corridor as he inched along, the flames roaring behind him.

In that tinder-box of a building, half tent

and half structure, the fire was spreading fast. There were flames in the hallway before the Kid reached the stairs. Getting down the steps was something to be remembered afterwards as a nightmare is remembered — hazy and horrible. But he made it. He came to the street just as part of the second story collapsed behind him, crashing downward thunderously while sparks shot toward the sky.

Men were still battling along the boardwalks and in the dusty channel between them. But hostilities ceased temporarily, nearly every eye turning toward the Golden Slipper where smoke billowed to hide the heavens. In the hush that fell, the Kid raised his voice. "The Three are dead — inside!" he shouted. "Your paymasters won't be payin' off for Central Western tonight!"

He saw two or three swollen jaws sag in surprise. He saw a half-dozen toughs take to their heels, a knot of shouting M.P. workers hard after them. Then Tyler Whitman was elbowing toward the Kid, supporting him, leading him away from the doomed saloon.

"That finishes it," the railroad builder said. "The telegraph wasn't destroyed. Those fellows just dragged O'Dade away from the key when he tried to warn us this morning. Loomis used the wire to get word to Fort Yellowstone. He's a government man, and his authority was great enough to impress the commander. Bluecoats are on their way here to declare martial law, but I guess we won't need them. The news got around, and the toughs have already begun to run out. And now The Three are dead, you say! That news will finish the rout."

"Then we've won!" the Kid babbled. "We've won!"

"Won?" Whitman echoed, and the Kid noticed that he was just as white and strained-looking as he'd been when they'd run that doomed tunnel.

"We've cleaned up Deadman," Whitman conceded. "There's some satisfaction in that. But we've lost, son — lost! Don't you see? Central Western will swear these toughs weren't on their payroll. The race will go on as before. C.W. is far behind, but they'll beat us now. We were licked for good when the tunnel went down. It'll take weeks to clear it out, and we're tied up until we do. We can't get a yard of steel out to the end of the line otherwise!"

For the span of a second the Kid looked into the crest-fallen face of this fighting railroad builder who'd been his brother's friend — this man who'd made the good fight against all the odds and fought on even when defeat had already overtaken him. Then the Kid began laughing wildly, deliriously.

"A tunnel!" he shouted. "Mister, I'll hand you a tunnel all roped and saddled and ready to ride! A ready-made tunnel that can be turned into a railroad tunnel in a tenth of the time it would take to clear out your man-made tunnel after that dynamite blast. And it will be a more direct route, too."

"What's this — ?" Whitman began.

"I would have told you all about it before," the Kid babbled on, "but the M.P. tunnel was already dug, and it didn't make much difference then. Besides, it was part of the story concerning Storm Herndon, the story I kept to myself. Ty, this tunnel's exactly what you want! Kurt Ormond must have known it when he looked over that country. But he was one of The Three — working against M.P. instead of for it."

Tyler Whitman regarded him queerly — doubt, astonishment, and a great elation having their successive turns in the railroad builder's eyes.

"Things are coming a mite fast for me,

boy," he said at last. "I'm just hoping you're not completely out of your head. Our men found the doctor, and he's down in my private coach working on Storm Herndon. He says the old gent is going to pull through, too, and he wants to operate on Storm as soon as the old gent is strong enough. He found something wrong with Storm's back when he examined him, something that's been slowly paralyzing him these past few months, but the doc is positive he can fix it. Now I think we'd better march *you* down there and have the doc look you over."

Whitman supported the Kid on one side, and Key O'Dade appeared out of nowhere to bolster Matt McGrath's faltering footsteps on the other. In this manner they made their way toward the railroad tracks. And triumph walked with the Kid along the dusty street of Deadman, for he'd fought through to the flaming finish and his work was nearly done.

This pace was far too slow to suit his mood, but that was because Tara was waiting in yonder coach. . . .

20.

When the day came that the Kid and Tara took all of a morning to climb to the high places, the snow had come and gone again from Montana. Here in the upper reaches of the Big Thunders there were occasional white patches still lingering, although the foothills were beginning to don their mantle of green, for spring ruled the land once more.

Upon a promontory the man and the girl sat their saddles, looking down into the valley below them where twin rails sparkled in the thin sunlight. Below them, too, were buildings, tiny and toy-like in the distance, glistening with their first coats of paint, for a ranch was there where none had been before. But it was the railroad that held the Kid's eyes, and Tara's as well, until finally her laughter rang out.

"I never see the railroad without remembering Dad's change of heart," she said. "And yet I always knew he was not as bitter as he pretended to be. He only needed an excuse to make his peace with

Tyler Whitman. When Whitman's train got him to the doctor in Deadman in time to save his life, he had his excuse. Especially since a railroad doctor did so much for him."

"Seems like a mighty long time ago," the Kid remarked gravely. "Times have changed some. Now The Three are dead and gone. Cisco Yawberry and his outfit are serving time in prison for that dynamiting job. And Central Western has given up completely. The last time I saw Ty Whitman, he told me they'd sold their Montana holdings to him for a fraction of their worth. The northern track that Central Western laid will be a spur of Montana-Pacific."

"You never say much about those meetings with Tyler Whitman," Tara observed pointedly.

The Kid smiled. "He made me another offer," he admitted. "A better one than the last. He's a persistent coot, Ty is. He can't get it through his head that I'd rather run a few dogies of my own than help run somebody else's railroad. But speaking of your dad — I've been wondering why he hasn't been to Hidden Valley lately."

Tara laughed again. "He's practically letting the crew run the H-in-a-Hat. Since he's well enough to get around again, he's spending more and more time in Deadman," she said. "I saw him there when I went into town for supplies the other day. Now that Key O'Dade has been stationed permanently at Deadman, he and Dad have struck up quite a friendship. And Dad's become a dyed-in-the-wool railroad man. Imagine that!"

The Kid shook his head.

"It's terrible the way those two have contaminated each other," the girl went on. "Number twenty-seven was ten minutes late, as usual, and Dad was positively fuming. 'Faith and it's a fine way to be runnin' a railroad!' he told O'Dade. And what do you suppose Key had to say to that? 'I reckon you're plumb right, Storm,' he agreed. 'I'll pile onto the telegraph and see if I can dab a loop on that maverick!'"

The Kid joined in her laughter, but his eyes were thoughtful as the sweep of his hand took in the valley below them. There the steel stretched from the east to the west, the rails following the valley's gentle curve until they blended with the distance and became part of it.

"It's finished," he said. "And it's already bringing a new day to the range. Look at how Caprock and Lazura and Deadman have all become cattle shipping points, building a real prosperity on the ruins of the boom-towns. There's Hellvation Hank's monument, Tara — the railroad. It makes me proud to think I had a hand in the building of it."

She looked at him long and tenderly, and the laughter went from her eyes to be replaced by a solemn sweetness.

"You think *that* is the thing you built," she asked softly, "that would make Hank the proudest of you?"

He shrugged. "What better thing?" he countered.

"Have you seen the latest edition of Thackery Weaver's paper? He's clamoring for folks to build a church mighty soon. He says that now that we have another fighting sky-pilot on the range, it isn't seemly for folks to be crowding into the little ranch-house he's just built in Hidden Valley in order to hear him read from Hank McGrath's Bible. And a lot of other folks are saying that it's just like having Hell-vation Hank back with us to have you here. You've built a new life for yourself, Matt. I think that's the thing Hank would have liked the most."

The Kid gave her speech his grave consideration. "The frontier has needed the man with the Book as well as the man with the gun," he observed. "I'd like to think that there's a place for a man who can handle both." He grinned his easy grin. "Besides, I had to make a few changes in myself, didn't I?" he added. "Wasn't no other way to convince your dad that his gal wasn't throwin' herself away on a worthless, wide-loopin', hell-bent gunhand!"

Her smile was invitation enough, and his arms went around her, and her lips, brushing his, were cool and sweet. The Gospel Kid, that tumbleweed who had at long last taken roots, kissed his bride and had his kiss returned. He held her close for a long, long time, humble before the miracle of her love for him. And his unspoken pledge was that he would try very hard always to be worthy of that love.

Somewhere in the distance a locomotive's whistle wailed, eerie and forlorn. The valley walls caught the mournful sound, toying with it until even the echoes finally faded into the thin silence of the high country. A hush, serene and peaceful, brooded over Hidden Valley. . . .

The employees of Thorndike Press hope you have enjoyed this Large Print book. All our Thorndike and Wheeler Large Print titles are designed for easy reading, and all our books are made to last. Other Thorndike Press Large Print books are available at your library, through selected bookstores, or directly from us.

For information about titles, please call:

(800) 223-1244

or visit our Web site at:

www.gale.com/thorndike
www.gale.com/wheeler

To share your comments, please write:

Publisher
Thorndike Press
295 Kennedy Memorial Drive
Waterville, ME   04901